BAD
COMPANY

MAX
BARRINGTON

This book is a work of fiction. Unless otherwise indicated, all the names, characters, businesses, places, events and incidents in this book are either the product of the author's imagination or used in a fictitious manner. Any resemblance to actual persons, living or dead, or actual events and/or places is purely coincidental.

For the love of my life,
my darling wife and my inspiration,
Lynette

Other Books By Max Barrington

Woolgar River Curse: Receiving a phone call announcing that you are the heir to a 70,000 acre cattle property that is complete with a five bedroom mansion would be like winning the Lotto. But to Gus and Lynette Teague, it was the beginning of a discovery into corruption, deceit, tragedy and murder. Was it really an 'Aboriginal Curse' on that property that caused the death of a family of five, or simply tragic events?

Task: I was looking to make a few dollars until my next work project started. "Check out the Air Tasking pages on Facebook," they said. An Australian road trip from Cairns to Darwin turns into Mystery, Intrigue and Life Threatening Danger

Dying to Find Gold:

Fossicking for Gold in Australia is a popular activity. But when Mick West's, best mate goes missing whilst on a fossicking trip The police suspect Mick of murder.

The New March:

It was a hot day in the Far Northern Coastal Australian Town.

The first thing that Mitchell wanted as he walked into the sleepy town's public bar was a cool drink.

The last thing that Mitchell wanted, was to kill five people inside that sleepy town's public bar.

The First Ten Years in Australia From a 10 year old ten pound pom

An Amazing story of a ten year old boys adventure of coming from England to Australia with his parents in 1959.

It tells of the family's ten moves to different New South Wales towns, within ten years, whilst his father sought work, from a ferry skipper to a quarry manager.

It, also tells of a determination, to succeed in a new environment.

A very moving, yet, such an interesting turn of events, of a real family, based on a true story.

Prologue

The year was 2016, the place was the Mareeba Police Station.

Police were interviewing two witnesses to a shooting murder at a remote area on the banks of the Mitchell River in Far North Queensland.

'Right, let me get this clear' exclaimed Detective Sergeant Cameron Jamison of the Mareeba CID, 'You were all at the camp on the river on the Saturday night at the Mitchell River with the intention of fishing on the property, you were all aware that you were trespassing'

'No!' Interjected David Barnes (Barnsy), 'They don't own the river, the river's not their land, we were camped on the dry riverbed'

'But to get to where you were you had trespassed, and to go fishing the next day you would be further trespassing', quipped the sergeant, 'Right? So you left the camp at five o'clock the next morning and then, tell me again what happened?

The Detective Sergeant was not at all happy with what these fellows were telling him. It seemed to change around a bit the more times that they told it, and he knew that he had to get it right.

The call had come in late the previous afternoon at five fifty four PM, that there had been a shooting out at a location on the Mitchell River, it had been witnessed by two of the missing man's friends.

The distance from the nearest police station at Laura to the location of the reported shooting was two hundred and thirty kilometres but, it was a one manned station and the Senior Constable in residence was away on that day, so the call went to the next nearest major station being Cooktown.

Two constables had been despatched that evening to travel the three hundred and seventy kilometres, on mostly unsealed roads, from Mareeba to the alleged shooting incident near the intersection of the Mitchell and Palmer Rivers.

Senior Constable Franko Casselis and Constable Owen Jones arrived at the address of the phone call at two AM the following morning. They had collected the caller, Terry Andrews who took him to the campsite on the river. They had arrived at the campsite at two forty seven AM and listened to what both the witnesses had to report about the shooting and their missing companion. They then secured the area and the witnesses and made a call via their satellite telephone to Mareeba Police Station.

Backup teams of police arrived the next morning from Mareeba and investigated the alleged shooting site.

Later that same day, police arrested David Watson and Stan Strauss and transported them to Mareeba Police Station for further questioning.

Terry Andrews and David Barnes were escorted to the Mareeba Police Station to furnish statements to the police on the events that had happened the previous afternoon.

David Barnes again told the Detective Sergeant that at about five thirty am on the Sunday morning, they had all walked along the river towards the homestead which was about a kilometre away and had separated to start fishing in the river, he explained that they liked to separate when fly fishing for Barramundi as it involved transversing up and down the river banks and you needed good space around you.

They had passed a couple of good looking gullies with creeks entering the river and then broke from the river and went over a slight rise and then crossed a track then back onto the river, they were all about one hundred or so metres away from each other and the missing group member, Mark, was last seen starting to go down onto a riverbed, he was wearing headphones that were connected to his mobile telephone that he was using as a music source of pre recorded music, he was the only one wearing headphones whilst fishing.

The other two of the group were on the opposite bank around a bend in the river and David Barnes had left Terry and had gone back down the rise towards the river when he heard the sound of a vehicle with a diesel engine and assumed it would be the property owner Stan Strauss so he quickly found a place to stay out of sight from the vehicle that was heading his way, he assumed the others would also hear the Landcruiser and take similar action which they did with the possible exception of one member, Mark, who was wearing headphones. Barnsy had seen the Landcruiser go along the track that they had crossed earlier and he could make out its occupants to be the owners of the property, Stan Strauss and David Watson, although he could not see Mark he knew more or less exactly where he was and he shuddered when he saw the vehicle stop and one of the occupants get from the vehicle with a rifle in hand and fire a shot towards where Mark would have been fishing.

Barnsy was about to bolt when the person re entered the vehicle and the vehicle made a detour down the rise towards the river, he waited and watched and although he could no longer see the vehicle he heard it stop and he heard another gunshot followed by some other indistinct sounds.

Barnes was out of there and kept the tree line between him and the vehicle so that he could not be seen.

Terry Andrews told of a similar story with the exception of only hearing the vehicle and the gunshots, he too as soon as he thought it was safe bolted into the bush but became somewhat lost.

It took him an hour or so to return to the camp to find Barnsy waiting for him, he didn't think that he seemed to look too worried about the events of the day as they were having a beer and a chat, he had casually asked him had he seen Mark and when he replied in the negative Barnsy said he should be back soon and added, 'I hope those pricks didn't shoot him.'

It seemed the general consensus with Barnsy and Terry Andrews that Mark should show up later but Barnsy had suggested contacting the police so Terry had driven their Nissan Patrol back to another nearby property that had a telephone and contacted the police and they were now at the Mareeba Police Station making statements.

It appeared to be a pretty straight case as far as the Detective Sergeant could see and he organised to detain the property owners and a search of the property.

Both Stan Strauss and David Watson denied even being in that area of their property that day and told police that they were in the other direction of where the police claimed that Mark had gone missing, they were marking and ear tagging calves at the cattle yards a long distance from there.

Extensive searches of the property failed to find Mark or his body, some items with signs of blood were found on the river bank and DNA from samples taken, later revealed it to be the blood of Mark Crampton.

A firearms license search had shown that Watson was licenced to hold a Tikka .270 Rifle and that Strauss was licensed to hold a Marlin 30-30 lever action repeating rifle and a Savage pump action shotgun.

A search of the homestead and the vehicles on the property could only find the Tikka .270 rifle that was licensed to Watson, Strauss had stated that his shotgun and rifle were in his bedroom, if they weren't, then he had no idea where they were.

Tests were performed on the clothing of Strauss and Watson for both blood and gunpowder residuals but none were found. They appeared in the Cairns Law Courts and were both found guilty of murder under circumstantial evidence as the body of Mark Crampton was never found.

They both pleaded their innocence but were both convicted to life imprisonment for the murder of Mark Crampton and in accordance with a new law that had recently been passed, 'No Body, No Parole' they would never be released unless they would reveal the location of Mark Crampton's body.

Some say that it was the fastest murder case on record in Queensland law, as far as the police were concerned it had been a pretty simple case based entirely on circumstantial evidence and they had successfully obtained a conviction for the murder.

Detective Sergeant Cameron Jamison was amazed at the result, he had warned the prosecutor that the evidence from the two prospectors was flimsy and seemed to change every time they repeated it. He was also doubtful about other physical evidence, or more the lack of it, that they were implying in this 'circumstantial' case but the prosecutor told him that the jury would not have knowledge of it and he doubted that the defence would pick up on it. 'Ah well', thought Jamison, 'A conviction is a conviction.'

The 'No Body, no parole' law was introduced into Queensland in 2015, this law would apply to Srauss and Watson.

• • • • • • • •

Strauss & Watson

David Watson was born on Watsonville Station in 1974. He was raised, educated and worked on the property all his life, he had one younger brother, by two years, who was also born and educated on Watsonville but who had decided at the age of sixteen to leave the property and move to Chillagoe, a small town, some one hundred and eighty kilometres to the South East.

His parents had taken up the lease of 400,000 acres just to the west of Mount Mulgrave on the Mitchell River where it is joined by the Palmer River, in 1968.

Benjamin and Doris Watson had both worked and had been married in the Wimmera District of the State of Victoria and worked a small property that produced wool from wethers when they had heard from a friend of a lease available in Far North Queensland.

They had decided to leave the cold behind and had sold their small property to their closest neighbour for a modest price.

Less than half of the money from the sale of the Wimmera property enabled the purchase of the Far North Queensland lease of 400,000 acres, or 161,874 hectares.

They were aware that the country was rough and that the cattle carrying capacity was around one head per fifteen hectares and that the accommodation on the property was pretty sparse.

The property also had a passive income from mining leases that were along the riverbanks.

Tragically both Ben and Doris Watson were drowned whilst attempting to drive through a river crossing in their Landrover in 1994.

David Watson was the sole heir in the wills of Ben and Doris. The younger brother of David, named Jeffrey, had been cut from the will once he had left home in 1992.

Stan Strauss was born in Innisfail in 1972, the only son of the local Police Sergeant and School teacher. Stan had entered into a life of being in trouble with the law for some reason or other but only in a minor capacity.

He had found work in the canefields and had saved his money until, at the age of 20, had enough money to buy a cattle property of 100,000 acres, 40,468 hectares, that adjoined the Watson's property.

For the two years before the tragic drowning of Ben and Doris, Stan had a great working relationship with them, they would assist him when required and he would assist the Watsons in return.

Upon David's inheritance of Watsonville, both he and Stan Strauss had decided to combine the properties and become fifty-fifty partners in Watsonville.

Both being fairly young at twenty and twenty two, they had decided to modernise the property and aimed to maximise beef production at Watsonville and had taken out a small loan using the property as collateral, with this money they had purchased two second hand Robinson R22 helicopters for mustering and hired pilots for the mustering periods until they had both become proficient in flying them. The helicopters, together with a system of fixed cattle races installed in strategic places around the property allowed for more efficiency, with a better yield of up to thirty percent, annual mustering using a total of only four people, rather than the usual twelve. A drawback of Aerial mustering was that it took a considerable time for the cattle to settle down before drafting and loading on transports.

Both Stan and David were annoyed that they seemed to be plagued with trespassers on their property, it was either camping, shooting, fishing or metal detecting but it seemed to be a consistent problem that they both took exception to and started to go out of their way to detect and remove trespassers from Watsonville.

They even used the helicopters to check out boundaries and favourite fishing holes looking for trespassers.

The biggest problem it seemed with trespassers was the lighting of fires that sometimes became uncontrollable and became bushfires, the rubbish left behind at fishing holes in the rivers and creeks and huge damage to the roads and tracks from people becoming bogged and recovering bogged vehicles, but what seemed worse of all, was the bullets zipping past them whilst they were working around the property.

They had become known for terrorising trespassing people and had been accused of taking overhead shots at them and rigging wires and other obstacles across gazetted roads. They had been visited by police on a number of occasions in respect to complaints from people merely travelling through their property on gazetted roads.

They, of course, denied any wrongdoing, and when confronted with bullet holes in vehicles, they blamed the shooters that came onto the property that seemed to fire indiscriminate shots anywhere and everywhere, hence that is why they were against roads throughout their lands being gazetted.

The police knew that Stan and David were not being truthful but they could not prove anything on them and only notes were recorded against the complaints that were received by the police.

But it seemed that the actions of the Watsonville Station owners were working and the roads became quieter as articles appeared in such publications of *Camping, 4wd Driving, Fossicking and Fishing,* with warnings to people travelling around the area of Watsonville Station.

It became well known in later years to avoid any roads in and around Watsonville and even council and electricity workers were known to take long detours around the property.

Annual Board Meeting 2015

'We are running out of development sites, it's as simple as that, we have taken just about all of the caravan and camping ground sites that have become available, we have bought council members of small rural communities and have gained their parks and reserves, we have bought up all the cane farms that have become available, I reiterate, we are running out of development sites in Queensland' the 'chair' for Juliet Consolidated Enterprise Proprietary Limited (JCE) had just announced at the company annual general meeting of its six directors.

JCE was a very successful development company that specialised in acquiring suitable land, or properties, for commercial or residential purposes. Its commercial development consisted of manufacturing and/or warehouse facilities at a suitable location or region that was considered prime for development.

JCE very rarely purchased the land or property but rather entered into a partnership, or deal, with the landowner and quite often another company would be formed to engage JCE as the developer.

This acquired region was then labelled as manufacturing decentralisation and the idea was either sold or implanted in the minds of the local council and chamber of commerce as yet another possible source of income.

This was often achieved by the careful selection of one or more councillors who may be sympathetic towards JCE in return for a possible future position with either JCE or one of its many offshoots or even become a benefactor of one of its surplus properties.

Following this, then various major Australian manufacturing or assembly companies were approached with the idea of relocation or decentralisation or even a new business opportunity with generous rebates on rates and charges available from the council, not to mention construction and capital gains assistance from the developer.

Once such a project was underway, a residential development would follow as the infrastructure would be there for employment.

The 'chair' was none other than the Queensland Premier, Ms Fiona Gibson, the daughter of the mining magnate Horace Rimshaw The other five directors of JCE in attendance were;

Mr Eric VanDerstatt a grazier from Toowoomba who was also a local councillor. Eric VanDerstatt was the founder of VanDerstatt Constructions a well known building construction company that was busily engaged in providing residences to many of JCE's development projects in various Australian States. Mr VanDerstatt was also the President of the Building Construction Association of Queensland, a voluntary building standards self regulator made up of its members who also formed a strong building materials buying group.

Doctor Christopher Dunwoody MLA (Lib) Qld was formerly a director of a Brisbane Hospital and the resident surgeon, he now spends most of his time enjoying life at one of his three Gold Coast Resorts where he resides with his wife. His two sons run the three resorts between them together with their wives.

Christopher enjoys being a Federal Member of Parliament and is currently 'The Speaker of the House'.

Roz Dagleish is a partner of Huey, Cheetham and Dagleish, Barristers and Solicitors that has chambers in almost every capital city in Australia. A good friend of Fiona Gibson, Roz was also once a colleague of Fiona when she was once a member of State Parliament and enjoyed being the Qld Attorney General.

She has many political and business interests in both Queensland and Western Australia. Accepted to the bar as a King's Council, but these days she is rarely seen in court.

Carl Stephenson formally the Queensland Police Commissioner, the resignation of Carl Stephenson, who once served as the Chief Superintendent of the Queensland Police and then later became commissioner, was triggered by allegations that lacked any credible evidence or corroboration.

Carl is the owner of several Queensland country hotels (pubs) and spends most of his time either at country race meetings or visiting one of his pubs.

Since retirement things have been hard for Carl as many of his so called friends turned their backs on him once he had lost his powers in the police force. Unlike the others, Carl relied heavily on his dividends from JCE and it showed.

The sixth and final director on the board was Father Damien Downes, an ordained priest who was now an administrator in the church's financial department and who also undertook church investments in the form of real estate and commercial ventures.

The church kept Father Damien out of the public eye these days due to some unfounded allegations of inappropriate language whilst conducting masses and condemning fellow priests with respect to very publicised unusual activities and he narrowly missed being charged, on a number of occasions, for physical assault on some of these priests. Father Damien did not seem to have a care in the world and lived in a luxury apartment in Brisbane's exclusive Teneriffe that was valued at over twenty million dollars, Father Damien shrugged that valuation off as a joke suggesting that one hundred and twenty thousand would probably pull it up. Father Damien enjoyed a drink and openly displayed this fact at board meetings by demolishing at least one full bottle of scotch whiskey.

That concluded the makeup of the Board of directors for JCE, the company that, generally, had a vision of at least ten years ahead was not looking good after the next five years as they seemed to be running out of viable areas of land and developers cannot develop without land.

True they had a very high criteria as far as properties went but they were also very open to diversification.

JCE had recently suffered a huge loss of some thirty seven million dollars through a failed project that would have been the saver in the five years that was now of contention. It was not unusual for JCE to suffer a loss from time to time but this particular one had hurt for two reasons, the huge amount of money lost with no possible salvage and secondly, there were no other projects to take its place to maintain the steady income stream.

The other five directors had their attention fixed on Fiona and were waiting with bated breath for the resumption of her announcement which they all knew would contain a solution to the issue at hand, but in this instance, instead, she fell silent.

'And the solution...........'? Asked Carl Stephenson.

'I was rather hoping that some of you may have some thoughts that you may want to expand with us all' was Fiona's response.

They just all looked at each other and did not appear to be too concerned, Fiona observed this and added,

'You may feel relaxed at the present, but in five years time when the dividends get smaller, or disappear, then you may feel very concerned. Sure, we may have a solution at the next meeting in a year's time, but we need to be onto it now!... Not in a year's time, at least start something in some direction today'.

'Diversification' Father Damien Downes suggested, 'We always seem to be looking at the same thing, either residential housing developments or commercial developments, what about something other than those'?

'Such as Father' smiled Fiona.

'He's right' uttered Roz Dagleish, 'We've done the housing development to death, it's been good to us but maybe it's time to change'?

'We have mentioned the greatest requirement that exists on earth in the past, but we have never pursued it' Father Damien answered.

'Enlighten me, please' Fiona was not a quick thinker, she didn't have to be in her position as Premier, she was just the figurehead, so to speak, she enjoyed advisors for all types of situations and had no requirement to be smart.

'I am talking *FOOD* madam, we have but briefly discussed it from time to time, but we have never really got very serious about it, we all agreed the world can't go on without it but we seemed to have totally ignored it'. Continued Father Damien.

'Are you talking 'Cereal Farming''? Asked Dr Dunwoody, 'could be good, but I think we might have left it a bit late though'.

'That yes and maybe livestock' was the Father's response.

'And why not the whole deal with abattoirs and butcheries?' Asked Roz becoming interested in the good Father's suggestion.

'Order..order, let's come to order, let someone put a motion forward' Fiona had regained the meeting and a motion was accepted to look into a food supply venture and Father Damien Downes had accepted to provide an indicative viability assessment on areas of food production for the next meeting.

The meeting came to a close and the bar was opened, the caterer was informed that dinner would be taken at six thirty that evening and Doctor Chris Dunwoody complimented Father Damien Downes on his excellent suggestion and offered to help in the viability research as he handed him a glass of scotch and ice.

Eric VanDerstatt was, understandably, not too happy that JCE would not be seeking an extensive construction type of future project as his company was starting to struggle to maintain its extensive knowledgeable team of project engineers and managers. Soon some of the better ones would be on a sizable retainer with no projects to oversee, he approached Father Damien and jovially suggested he concentrate on a project that would be without any infrastructure so they could start from the ground up.

'Much too early to even consider what I am seeking Eric'

'I suppose that I mean,..we don't want to look at buying someone out to improve an established food chain, you know'? Added Eric.

'Do you have any ideas on what we should be looking for, Eric'?

'No, but I do have some good scout contacts in the Western Australia broad acre farming regions, they would know who is doing it hard and they could analyse them for you'.

'I was looking more towards the frontier of Far North Queensland', but Father Damien was rudely interrupted by Carl Stephenson,

'There's fuck all up that way old son'!

A silence descended on the room as it was a strict protocol that swearing would not be tolerated at meetings.

The 'Dinner Gong' sounded.

'Saved by the bell old chap' beamed Dr Dunwoody as they gathered towards the dining room where the traditional board meeting 'Roast Beef' was being served with traditional baked vegetables and horseradish sauce.

Carl Stephenson was sitting next to Father Damien and Father Damien was receiving an uninvited report on the state of conditions in the Far North

Queensland territory with advice on staying away from the area as it was a disaster waiting to happen,

'I tell you the Queensland Department of Agriculture has rated the cattle production north of The Palmer River at around fifteen hectares per head' Carl enlightened the good Father, 'Which, that alone, puts a halt on any grazing in the area, not to mention the huge costs associated with mustering the cattle and transporting them to the nearest markets. Do not even consider the area, Father'.

'I remember reading about you and your drug operations around that area' exclaimed Roz Dagleish, 'All rather colourful I thought'.

'And all above board Madam, I can assure you, we broke up a huge cultivation ring up there that had apparently been running for many years undetected' replied Carl.

'Yes and I'll bet it's still happening up there too' added Doctor Christopher Dunwoody.

'I know it is Chris, believe me, but until you see just how wild and extensive the country is out there then you have no idea, the country is just so vast and now with modern technology, the cops get busted by satellite detectors as soon as they go on to a property and the cultivators are long gone into hiding by the time the crops are discovered. It takes about a week or so to collect the crops and destroy them on site with a huge contingent of men and three weeks later the cultivators have a new crop coming up. It's just impossible'.

Carl went on to tell of one occasion where the police used their drones in an attempt to locate the offenders on one of these plantations but the perpetrators were in possession of much better technology than that available to the police at the time and they took out the police drones by overriding the drones communication systems,

'The drones just dropped from the sky' he said

More than one of the directors were of the opinion that Carl Stephenson seemed to be going to great depths to turn Father Damien away from Far North Queensland and of course made a joke out of it.

'Sounds like you still have a strong interest in the plantations up there Carl' suggested Fiona, 'Should we be looking at getting into cultivating up there'? This created laughter around the table and soon the subject was forgotten, much to the relief of   Carl Stephenson.

Following dinner, Carl did offer his help to Father Damien and implied that with his extensive local knowledge of the area, it could make things a lot easier with his assistance, but Father Damien firmly declined his assistance and assured him that he had a very capable person on hand to undergo a complete feasibility study of that area.

'During the after dinner drinks, Carl maintained a pleasant conversation with Father Damien which after some time revealed the name of Father Damien's exploration scout to be a Mark Crampton and other than him running a market analytics company based in Canberra nothing else was revealed of him.

The meeting, dinner and evening drinks had concluded and all had agreed on the date for the following month's meeting.

The following morning the official JCE manager was instructed to appoint Mark Crampton of MCA (Mark Crampton Alanyctics) with a charter to survey and perform a feasibility study in an area north of The Palmer River where it meets with The Mitchell River on a broad range of activities from mining to food production and to report directly to the board of JCE, the tenure was for twelve months.

Father Damien Downs had commenced his task issued by the board.

● ● ● ● ● ● ● ●

Mark Crampton

Mark Crampton had received the email from the JCE manager and had no idea what it was about, he reread it for the third time;

Mr Mark Crampton

MCA Pty Ltd, Canberra ACT.

I have been instructed by the board of directors of Juliet   Consolidated Enterprises Pty Ltd, to confirm your appointment for the purpose of conducting a feasibility study as per the attached scope of purpose and topographical maps.

A full brief is enclosed for your perusal, if you require any additional information please contact Fr Damien Downes on 049951014.

The tenure for this study is twelve months at the agreed remuneration, including all expenses and associated costs, of six hundred thousand dollars, fifty percentum of that value will be deposited in your nominated bank instantly and the balance after completion.

Mark had never heard of JCE and had no idea what the letter meant other than the six hundred thousand dollars, but he certainly knew who Father Damien Downes was as he dialled the number listed on the mail.

'Hello, Father Downes speaking'

'What the fuck is going on 'Damo'?

'Ahh…Mark, I was just about to give you a call to warn you about the email, but it seems I might be too late'

'Yeah, I just got it, but what does it mean'?

'Mate, a little job came up at the board meeting and naturally, I just thought of you as I know you are at loose ends just now, Father Damien explained to Mark.

Mark Crampton had been the victim of sexual abuse at Saint Edward's Boys College, Canberra in his early teen years as a boarding student.

As it happened a Bishop was visiting the college and Mark and his friend George had been selected by the college to become the Bishop's personal assistants during his stay. Unfortunately, the Bishop had taken the opportunity to abuse Mark and Mark had vigorously fought off the Bishop's advances and had threatened to go to the police to make an official complaint.

Father Damien was the physical education teacher at the college at that time and was very popular with the boys as he was also the school team's rugby league coach and he not only turned a blind eye to the boys smoking and drinking but also joined them in the occasional drink and smoke.

Fortunately, Mark had told Father Damien all about the incident and Father Damien was able to persuade Mark not to report the matter to the police and that he would ensure that Mark would be well compensated in return, he also promised Mark that the Bishop would be well and truly punished for his actions, much more so than the consequences of reporting the Bishop to the police. Mark reluctantly agreed to keep the incident quiet and to act as if nothing had happened.

It was a very strained week for Mark to pretend that nothing had happened and finally, the Bishop's last day visiting at the college had arrived. A farewell dinner was planned for the Bishop aboard the floating restaurant, MV City of Canberra.

It was known that the Bishop was not feeling well due to the choppy water conditions on the lake that night and had visited the restrooms which are located out on the rear lower deck.

Indeed it was Father Damien Downes who had assisted His Grace to the restroom where he had left him in private to recover from his bought of illness.

It was about an hour after he was last seen going towards the restroom with Father Damien that the alarm was raised that His Grace was in fact, not in the restroom, he seemed to have disappeared and a search of the boat failed to locate him. The ACT Water Police were immediately notified and a search of the area the next morning revealed his body floating in Lake Burley Griffin, such a tragic accident.

The church although saddened by this tragic event was also somewhat relieved as the stories about the

Bishop were becoming too numerous and it was becoming harder to suppress the reports of child abuse by the Bishop.

The Arch Bishop was shocked at what Father Damien Downes was telling him and asked him to repeat himself,

'If it pleases your Grace', Father Damien with confident composure again settled in the visitor's chair that was placed in front of the Arch Bishop's desk, 'I do have first hand evidence of the Bishop's activities during his visit to Canberra and also a full dossier of the Bishops previous sexual abuses on students'. The last part was a lie, he had only heard of rumours but the Arch Bishop would not know that.

'And you feel a reward of twenty five million dollars for advising the church, and *no* other persons or entities of these activities, would be in order'?

'Yes, I do your Grace' Father Damien replied calmly.

'The office will be in touch with you Father, you are excused', were the last words that Father Damien ever heard from the Arch Bishop. The Arch Bishop's office contacted him the following day seeking his banking details.

On the day following the Bishop's disappearance, Mark had developed the utmost respect for Father Damien and they had remained very good friends and had stayed in contact.

Father Damien was forever giving gifts to Mark such as cars and even an apartment and Mark knew enough to not ask any questions.

Mark now listened intently to what 'Damo' was saying to him, true he was at loose ends. Following college he had applied to the Australian Defence Force Academy to become a fighter pilot with the Australian Airforce, he attended and passed the YOU session, the assessment session, the officer selection board and finally the Flying training school at at Williamtown, just north of Newcastle, this training course which he completed together with a degree in physics, in around four years only to discover that he suffered chronic air sickness and was unable to continue training as a jet pilot but could continue as a military drone analyst and controller, same as being a pilot, they said, except you don't leave the ground.

Mark had continued in drone analytics and found it very challenging, especially when a drone failed to destroy its target.

Once a drone failed on a mission a full examination of the mission was analysed and scrutinised.

Why? Did the mission fail, had the drone arrived at the destination on time, if the answer was no, then a check of all four motors was conducted starting with the electrical supply rate measured to each motor, the revolutions of each motor, the pitch of the rotor blades. The wind speeds and directions, the moisture content of the atmospheric pressure.

Everything about that drone flying on that mission was double checked to ascertain if the drone had been where it was calculated to be at the time that it should have been there.

Once that had been checked then it was onto the weapons function, was the projectile's coefficiency checked, was the charge a tested component, was the ignition spontaneous, and check and check and check, until a solution appeared which was in most cases some minor item that had caused the mission failure. Such causes were found to be a slight difference in rotor speed to cause the aircraft to cause drag to one side and that the automatic yawl compensator would correct this but in doing so may cause a slight lag in airspeed to lose a millisecond in coordination time when the projectile is fired to cause the projectile to miss its target.

It was when no such instances of malfunction could be detected, then a complete takedown and analysis of the drone was required.

It was during one such scrutiny that revealed a component of the drone's motherboard was extraneous to its ADF specification, in other words, this drone had something other than that of its Australian Defence Force Specification fitted to the drone.

After extensive investigation, it could only be assumed that the Chinese manufacturer of the drone had placed a device into the drone to report back the drone's location and flight data but was only activated when the drone was at cruising height and speed. This would report the drone's direction and possibly its target.

It was not believed that the device could interfere with the drone's operational functions, it was simply a reporting device, a spying device.

All other drones were immediately checked to find several of the newer model drones were also equipped with this device.

A solution to remove the device was established as a priority and all new drones being received from the drone manufacturer were also found to be fitted with this device.

It was decided by the ADF in conjunction with ASIO (Australian Intelligence Organisation) not to approach the Chinese manufacturer of the drones in this instance as it was assumed their response would be, that the device was merely a quality assurance tool for possible future device failure.

By not advising the manufacturer and by building an add on to the drones operational application, the ADF was able to use a drone fitted with this device as a decoy to anyone that was monitoring the drone to assist in any future drone missions.

This meant that if someone monitoring the drone was advising a group of an impending drone attack, they would be advising an all clear, or stand down, situation as the drone was off course to the target, but the drones without the device fitted would be on target for an imminent attack.

As things went quiet on the international front and the US Military had pulled out from Afghanistan, Mark had decided to opt out of the airforce, he didn't really need to be working on 'scenario' cases rather than real ones and definitely did not need to be regimented any longer.

He had gained a degree in physics and had acquired great analytical skills, he was sure to find some sort of work.

A close friend of Mark's late father, who had been like a second father to Mark since his father's tragic death when Mark was only nine years of age, had come up with a suggestion that Mark should start his own company as a business analyst as there seemed to be a call for them in these harsh commercial times and as fate would have it, another friend of his who owned a Pioneer Plasterboard Franchise at the South Coast of NSW was losing such an amount of money at the franchise that he was considering closing it down. Mark may be able to assist by looking at the company's operation and checking it for obvious flaws.

Mark would have nothing to lose and it would also help out his friend. Mark took on the job and even though he knew nothing of business acumen, or very little, the Air Force had taught him analytical skills that he could apply to how this business was being run.

It was quite a simple situation with the plasterboard franchise that it was stupid, the manager engaged to run and operate the business was obviously a fool when it came to common sense trading. Mark likened him to the two brothers who bought watermelons from a farmer for $2 each, they set up a stall by a busy road and sold them for $2 each, at the end of the day they calculated their sales and one brother said to the other;

'Didn't make much money today, what do yer reckon we should do'?

'Get a bigger truck,' answered the other brother.

And that is exactly what this franchise manager was doing, as his price was so competitive and he had great volume sales of plasterboard he had also employed extra staff and paid overtime to get the high volume of the product out, but he had not considered his trading costs and sadly the franchise ended up closing.

It had been a great experience for Mark but had resulted in very little money for him in return for his efforts as the owner had little money left following his venture into Plasterboard.

Mark now worked as a casual coach driver doing Canberra to Sydney Express three times a week for three hundred dollars a trip and it suited his lay back sort of lifestyle. Three days of work and four days off was just perfect, he could work up to seven days if he wanted but he declined the offers from the bus company.

On the days that he didn't work he would eat out at different restaurants and bistros and soon discontinued going to the places where the food was either pretentious or just plain shit.

It amused him to watch people, especially lunchtime groups usually made up from, he guessed, office workmates who would buy exotic foods, that they could not afford, and pretend to eat them with relish. The most obvious were the oyster eaters who simply swallowed them without ever getting a taste of them.

Mark would spend at least one day each two weeks, cleaning his unit, or more accurately Father Damien's unit, as it was not yet in Mark's name, Damo kept on saying 'Must get that transferred' but he never seemed to get around to it.

It was a large, three bedroom, three bathroom unit with a large kitchen, formal dining room, family room and very comfortable lounge. Mark kept two of the bedrooms and bathrooms closed as with the dining and family rooms, he didn't need such a big unit, Damo had some stuff in one of the bedrooms and he would, very, occasionally come down to Canberra for a visit but he never stayed for too long as it was either too cold or too hot for him and he would always comment, that he didn't know how he once lived here?

• • • • • • • •

'You only have to study the area before you go and make a plan, get up there and just look around in that area as nominated and find out what's happening, for fucks sake Mark, you are not an idiot, you are an educated man and you know what JCE is looking for out there, just do it, Mark'. Father Damien was convincing Mark quite easily.

Looking at the maps, the areas to the north of the Palmer and the Mitchell Rivers don't reveal the rough and harsh terrain. It was evident to Mark that the best base would be Cooktown but it would be a six to seven hour drive, depending on the road conditions, from Cooktown to the intersection of the rivers which would mean having to camp out somewhere.

Mark added to his growing list of items 'Camper Trailer', he already had a Landcruiser 70 series dual cab utility at the start of the list and now he would research camper trailers to find a suitable one as well as various items of camping gear, his list was now looking at around the one hundred and fifty thousand dollar mark which left him half of his advancement left for fuel, food, other accommodation and other consumables.

The following morning Mark was at the ACT Toyota dealer looking for a 70 series dual cab and as fate would have it they could offer a Merlot Red model that had diff locks, tow bar, high lift body kit, UHF radio and heaps of other accessories including a lock up metal canopy that was also painted in Merlot Red, it was a demonstration model and had only twelve thousand kilometres on the speedo and they were keen to do a deal of around ninety six thousand dollars and offered Mark and excellent price for his Tesla.

Next was a camper trailer, he had in mind what he wanted but when he had looked at a few he was losing interest, they were just too much work to set up and back again but when he saw the MDC X10E which presents as a small compact caravan with everything that he would need he changed his mind from camper to a small caravan, plus it had a much more comfortable bed. By the end of the following week, he had everything that he thought he would need and was ready to head north.

David Barnes

Meanwhile, Carl Stephenson had left a message for Kirill Nikolaev, 'Nick' on his home phone near Gladstone in Queensland, to contact him as soon as practicable. He did not have a mobile number for Nick, the system was, according to Nick, he leave a message on the landline number and Nick would get back to him either sooner or later. Each time that Nick had called him back it was on a different mobile number.

David Barnes had spent fifteen of his thirty three years in Far North Queensland. He had left his birthplace of Martha Cove on the Mornington Peninsula in Victoria, along with his parents, to seek a better lifestyle, and also to get the Victorian Police off his back for minor drug offences. He had chosen to head north for no other reason than a friend of his fathers was driving a 'B Double' truck from Dandenong to Townsville and a lift was available.

Townsville had not appealed to David with its dry tropical climate and after only a few days he ventured along the coast north to Cairns spending a few months along the way at Tully and Mission Beach.

Finally arriving at Cairns broke with nowhere to stay he met up with two young deckhands, Adam and Troy, at Gilligan's Backpackers in the city. They had told David about the good conditions on board the prawn trawlers and although it was short, seasonal work, the pay was good enough, sometimes depending on the catch, to last over until the following season. Plus, you get accommodation and meals.

They had explained that the Banana prawn season would be starting next week at the end of March and would go to mid June. There would be a break for about a month until the Tiger prawn season would start from August to September. Now was the time to get on a boat if he could find one and they told him that their boat had a full crew but other boats were still taking on crew and where to look for work.

He was on the wharf at Portsmith, the Cairns waterfront area, early the next morning with his possessions in one small backpack and was lucky enough to get a berth on the prawn trawler 'Rag Top', an independent twenty two metre long trawler with a crew of seven and about to head to Bamaga later that morning.

Rag Top's skipper was a huge Isander looking man with maybe a little Malayan added with the name of Isaya.

He had told David, in no uncertain terms, that he would be paid very little until he was useful, and that if he was of no use to the trawler, then he would be put ashore in either Bamaga or Karumba. The choice was his, take it or leave it?

Rag Top had left Cairns at ten thirty that morning with a strong south easterly wind causing a two metre swell, by the time Rag Top was north of Port

Douglas David was lying on the stern deck as sick as a dog.

'You are not on the payroll until you can work 'Barnsy' and that goes for your tucker and bunk too, so I'll have to deduct your board from your pay until you can work, OK?' Isaya told David.

David could only nod his head in agreement, he wasn't game enough to open his mouth for fear of another bout of vomiting.

By the time they had reached Bamaga, two days after leaving Cairns, David, or now 'Barnsy', as everyone called him, was feeling much better and the trawler's cook, Chongy, assured him that he would now have his sea legs and that he would cook fish chop suey for dinner tonight and it was guaranteed a tonic for weak sea legs.

Rag Top was running a prawn trawl double rig with one 'warp wire' on each of the booms on either side of the vessel. These warp wires led to a bridle that connected to the otter boards that were designed to keep the nets open like a funnel. The ground gear, made from heavy chains that are connected to the bottom edge of the net causes the net bottom to skim over the seabed and encourages prawns living on the sea floor into the trawl mouth of the net.

While the trawl was down Barnsy was put to work cleaning the hopper and the sorting tables, when the first trawl came up he was shown how to sort bycatch and to allow the prawns through to the prawn sorting belt, he was then shown how to sort the prawns and what to identify to eject unsatisfactory prawns and then how to perform dipping of the prawns into the solution of metabisulphite prior to packing and freezing.

Prawning was more complex than David had thought and he found it interesting but hard work, by the end of the day he was looking forward to knocking off but that didn't happen. The crew had their evening meal while the trawl was down and then it was back into bringing up the trawl and sorting under the halogen arc lights that are placed above the working deck.

Sleep was taken in shifts by the crew and the prawning continued all night and into the next day until the nets came up almost empty and then it was off to another fishing ground searching for prawns.

After two weeks the trawlers freezer was full and David assumed that they were now heading back to Cairns to unload the catch and it was back to lazy days of net mending.

To David's dismay, the Rag Top was rendezvousing with a barge to offload the catch for transit to Cairns and then it was back to the twenty four hour shifts.

Rag Top was in the Gulf for just over two months and had made a monster haul in prawns much to the crew's delight as it meant a big pay packet of about sixteen thousand dollars for the two months of work, about two thousand dollars per week.

They would now return to Cairns and the trawler would be readied to head back for the Tiger prawn season which was twice as long as the Banana prawn season that they had just completed and Isaya invited 'Barnsy' on for the Tiger season.

Other than David, there were only three of the Banana season crew aboard the Rag Top when it left Cairns for the Tiger prawn season and three new crew members, they still had the same skipper, Isaya, and the cook, Chongy, along with, Grumpy Bob. Of the new crew, one was a large muscly Pommy who seemed to complain quite a lot and had a run in with Isaya, who threatened to put him off at Bamaga if he 'didn't pull in his head'.

It was about two months into the season and the Pommy's whinging was getting worse, he was getting on everyones nerves, his voice was starting to make David nauseous and he would not stop talking. It was during the night trawls that suddenly David seemed to realise that the Pommy had stopped talking and after a while noticed that the Pommy was not with him on the sorting table but had been replaced by Grumpy Bob.

'Where's the Pommy?' David asked Bob.

'He's in the head, he's crook'. Was Bob's unemotional answer.

It wasn't until about ten o'clock the next morning that David, noticing that the Pommy was still not present at the sorting table again spoke to Bob,

'Is the whinging prick still sick, Bob'?

'Fucked if I know, just shut up and do your fucking work. It's not good to ask too many questions on a trawler'. Bob seemed unphased.

It was later that afternoon when Isaya announced to everyone on board that it looked like the Pommy must have fallen overboard during a trawl at some stage last night and that he had conveyed a message to the barge who would convey a message to the police at Bamaga and that we would be spending the rest of the afternoon and evening searching for the 'man overboard', the Pommy.

To David, it did not seem to him, like searching, more just like prawning with Isaya occasionally flashing the spotlight around on the water.

 David could not help himself and said to Bob,

'Wouldn't it be better to stop prawning for a while and head back to where we were last night?'

'Suggest that to Isaya mate, and we'll be looking for you tomorrow' grinned Bob and it suddenly dawned on David that the Pommy had gone missing by design. It didn't pay to have a run in with the skipper on a prawn trawler.

When the police interviewed the crew at Bamaga a few days later it seemed that David was the last one to see the Pommy.

'He was working with me on the table one minute, and then the next time I looked up, he was gone!' David had truthfully told the police.

David stayed on board the Rag Top for three full seasons of each Banana and Tiger prawns and had saved over two hundred thousand dollars from prawning alone.

There had been no more loss of people onboard the Rag Top but two other trawlers had reported losses of a total of three deckhands who had gone missing, presumably, fallen overboard.

It was on his last, and final, prawning trip that he met up with a new deckie on board Rag Top, Terry Andrews from New Zealand. Terry had just been released from prison where he was serving an eight year term for cultivating and supplying drugs.

Terry had bitterly complained to David after he had received his first pay for two months' work of only sixteen thousand dollars and had explained to David that he could make this amount of money in a week by harvesting Coca and turning it into cocaine. David was instantly interested and wanted to know more about this crop.

They spent many hours on that last return trip to Cairns on board Rag Top, talking about setting up a plantation and that they would look for a suitable place as soon as they got back on shore at Cairns.

Terry was aware of an area just north of where the Palmer River meets with the Mitchell River it was rugged and the natural vegetation would camouflage a crop from the satellite surveillance used by the police and water was in abundance.

He had also been warned that the area formed part of a four hundred thousand acre cattle property that was owned by a man named Stan Strauss who was renowned for going out of his way to find trespassers on his property.

Terry had got to know some members of a Russian bike gang whilst he was serving his term. The gang operated many illicit businesses from near Gladstone in Queensland. They had told Terry that, if he was ever interested in growing for them up north, they would teach him how to cultivate a product from Coca and would buy as much as he produced. They had given him a landline phone number to leave a message on if he was ever interested.

Terry had also learned from another source that it may be possible to buy a mining lease in that area to give him an excuse for being there. This person had also given Terry the address of a gold buyer in Cairns who may know of any mining leases for sale in that area.

'What do you's want the lease for?' The man at the shop that was selling metal detectors, fossicking equipment, topographical maps and books on how to find gold and other mining items. 'Do yous want it for growing drugs or looking for gold?'
Both David and Terry looked at the man in horror.

'You's don't have to look too shocked', said the shop owner. 'That's what they do up there, it's either fucking drugs or gold, you wouldn't be the only dicks growing Hemp or Coca and setting up a lab, or do you's think you've invented something new? Come on, show some fucking respect'.

They bought one of the five mining leases that was available and it was carefully selected by viewing a topographical map of the area situated on the cattle property that appeared to give good cover from vegetation, water and remoteness.

A bargain they thought at Nineteen thousand dollars and the shop owner wished them luck and grinning, said,

'If you should accidentally find some gold, bring it in and I'll give you a fair price for it'.

A rough map showing how to get to the lease, along with a couple of keys for gates and the shed at the lease, was issued to them and they set about organising to buy a reasonably good four wheel drive vehicle and some camping gear before setting out to find their new lease.

Although the lease was approximately six hundred kilometres from Cairns it seemed that it would be an all day trip to get there from Cairns by travelling via Mareeba, Lakeland and Laura. Although they set off early in the morning they were still around one hundred, or so, kilometres from their lease at four o'clock that evening and decided to camp along the track on that first night. That was the night that they met the landowner of their lease Stan Strauss and his partner David Watson.

'And what the fuck do you jokers think you are doing here?' Came a voice from behind them in the treeline that was close to the road. 'And,… you can put out that fucking fire before you fuck off out of here'.

'I can explain' Terry quickly responded. 'We have a mining lease on this property and that is where we are heading'.

'Is that so? Well, you are not on any lease here pal so get moving'.

David then butted in, 'Settle down mate, let us explain' but was cut off by Strauss,

'I'm not your mate! Now fuck off before I get serious'.

That was enough for Terry, he was tired from driving all day and most of it had been on extremely rough tracks, he didn't need this.

'Just fucking calm down and stop being a fuckwit' was Terry's reply and as he said that he could see that this person was carrying a rifle, but unfazed went on. 'Just who the fuck are you anyway, even if we are trespassing you have no right to threaten us like you are'.

The man in the shadows moved closer to Terry and David and not sounding quite as authoritative said that he was the owner of the property and that he was fed up with people trespassing on his land. Terry and David assured him that they were not intending to trespass and assumed it was a gazetted road they were travelling on which gave them a right for passage.

'The stupid council think that it is a gazetted road but I can assure you fellows that it is not, I'll let you camp here tonight but make sure you put the fire out properly when you leave tomorrow and in future.....let me know if you need to camp on my land'.

'You're a fucking joke mate' Terry had had a gutful of this bloke and wasn't afraid of him, 'We don't even know who the fuck you are, let alone your fucking contact number, grow up mate'!

'The contact number should be on your lease agreement'. Quipped Strauss sounding even less unsure, he wasn't used to people standing up to him and he didn't like it.

'We haven't even had time to read the fucking lease agreement', added David, 'Don't worry we'll be gone at first light'. With that, the man in the shadows, and the person with him, turned around and went into the trees where they could no longer be seen. A short time later David and Terry heard a diesel engine start and then they heard the sound of a vehicle on the dirt road heading away from them.

'What a fucking arsehole' mumbled David getting a couple of beers from the car fridge.

'Well, that's what those blokes in Cairns were telling us about, that prick doesn't worry me, mate, fuck him, at least he'll keep others away from our lease'. And they both laughed a relief as they drank their beers.

They found their lease the next morning and had used the keys they had been given to unlock the gate, there was another padlock connected to the padlock that their key operated and they assumed it belonged to the station owner whom they had met last night. Terry made a mental note to get rid of the other padlock.

Another key on the ring opened the front door of the shed that was located next to a roller door, it was very dark inside the shed but David found his way to the inside of the roller door, unlocked and then raised it so that it was fully open and allowed them to see inside the shed.

It was a standard looking six metre by six metre pressed metal shed with a corrugated iron roof, there was a very rough concrete floor which appeared to have been made from river gravel from the huge creek bed close to the shed. There was an old cast iron cooking range on one side of the shed with its chimney of unprotected sheet metal pipe going up through the roof. A small table with four chairs was beside a kerosine refrigerator and a set of concrete laundry sinks, or wash troughs, were set on besser concrete blocks. Three beds were at various locations around the shed as were various items of equipment including picks, shovels and a maddock. A Honda 2kva generator was beside the concrete wash troughs and looked to be quite new.

Another door at the rear of the shed and to the right hand side revealed a second shed of about half the size of the first that ran, sideways along the back of the main shed. This too had a roller door to the right hand side but it was too dark to go in and open it and Terry had to go and get the LED lantern that they had bought.

The lantern showed the smaller shed to contain even more mining and sluicing equipment including another generator and a small front end loader, a coil of rope, three 44 gal fuel drums, three 9kg gas bottles, two Honda powered pumps and various other equipment including four folding tables. Terry opened the roller door on the smaller shed to allow them to see the equipment in daylight.

'Better than what I thought' stated David.

'This'll make a good processing shed' said Terry nodding at the smaller shed, 'I'll see if I can get this fridge working to keep our beer cold and then we'll get this loader out and see if it works, it will come in handy'.

A busy day exploring and getting set up for camping in the shed and then to the planning of getting a crop happening.

Terry had already established a source of Coca Erythroxylum seeds and they would plant these in small plastic pots of approximately fifty millimetres in diameter using a quality potting mix and once watered and fertilised, these would be placed into small zip tie plastic bags which would be opened up and watered twice a week until they have sprouted, usually within one to two months, these can then be planted around a sunny protected area amongst other vegetation but will require watering every day. For this, an irrigation system would be required. A pump at the creek where previous dredging had taken place would be an ideal spot for pure, chemical free, water which the plants would thrive on.

Planting the seedlings out, amongst other vegetation, would also help camouflage the plants in their later growth as it would be unlikely that anyone would even notice what species the plant was, in fact it would only be recognised by a person who was familiar with the plant, to most it would resemble only a wild blackberry bush.

Terry and Barnsy were heading to Cooktown the next morning to buy a car box trailer from a local manufacturer and to source some irrigation equipment. It was Friday early afternoon when they arrived following the four hundred and fifty kilometre drive of mainly bush tracks and roads.

They collected and paid for the trailer which the manufacturer had also registered for them and then they collected other items that they had on their list.

They booked into the Central Hotel on Charlotte Street and enjoyed a few beers and a meal, they had gone to their room at around seven pm to get some rest before their planned early start of two am the following morning.

By two fifteen the next morning they were at the Cooktown Country Club green keepers workshop and store and were busy loading irrigation fittings and coils of water pipe onto their new trailer by torchlight.

By three am that same morning they were breaking into the Cooktown Garden Centre and loading pot plants and bags of potting mix and fertiliser onto their trailer and by four am that morning they were on their way back to their mining lease.

It would take a full twelve months before the plants could be lightly harvested of leaves and the fruits would be collected to retrieve the coca seeds which would be propagated in the same way as they had started from scratch.

Twelve months went very quickly as they had found so much to do around the lease. They had found some good fishing areas around the property that they had now discovered to be called Watsonville, it was named after the original owners of the property and Stan Strauss's partner in the property, David Watson was a descendant of the original owners.

They had encountered Strauss a number of times within the first twelve months that they were living on the mining lease at various locations on *his* property, Watsonville.

On every occasion, although Barnsy and Terry attempted to be friendly, and they were hoping to establish some form of a mutual relationship with

Strauss, it just did not happen and resulted in an altercation between them and Strauss with Strauss threatening to have them charged for trespassing and Terry challenging Strauss to a fight and telling him to fuck off before he gets hurt.

After a while, the boys thought it was quite amusing to have a Mexican Standoff, type of situation, with Strauss, though they were very wary of him nonetheless.

They had tried using the gold dredge and pump that they had found in the shed but found the work very hard for such a small return and had bought metal detectors from the gold buyer in Mareeba. These had proven to be both interesting and profitable and they wandered along the creeks and river beds finding some good nuggets and some junk like remains of old tins and odd metal items, even out in the middle of nowhere.

●　●　●　●　●　●　●　●

It was almost time for their first harvest and they had bought a Childs canvas, wading pool with an aluminium, bolt together frame, and had it set up in the small shed as their mulching area for the leaves. The selected leaves were then placed into the wading pool and with the aid of a whipper snipper, the leaves were mashed into a pulp, the pulp was gathered and placed onto the fold up tables that had been placed together and the extract was squeezed by hand from the pulp and placed in the sun to dry on another table.

The final result of their first yield was just under two kilos of the white powder and they sold it to their Russian friends for three hundred and sixty thousand dollars, less their minder fees', as they were called of twenty five percent.

They were quite happy with their first result which gave them an annual salary for each of one hundred and eighty thousand dollars, much better than a deckie on a prawn trawler and much less work.

Selling the product to the Russians seemed a complex operation, and they could only sell up to one hundred thousand dollars at a time, their first yield had to be sold in four transactions.

The only way to contact Nik was to call him on a number that he had supplied to them and let the number ring three times then hang up and Nik would contact them generally within an hour. The sale of the product was strictly only on the third day of every month between ten o'clock and noon they should contact the number and wait for the callback. They would tell the caller the weight of the product and the caller would tell them where and when to drop off the product.

Sometimes it was Cooktown, sometimes Cairns or Mareeba and even in between the major towns.

The product was packed into a laptop bag that had been supplied to them by Nik and the drop off was normally in a pub, club or busy cafe, they would go to exactly where they had been told and a person with an identical laptop bag that contained the payment, less the minder fee, in cash for the product, would be waiting, it was then simply a matter of exchanging the laptop bags.

It seemed that it could be a good lifestyle but they had to watch out for Strauss who was becoming more and more prominent around their mining lease area.

The small harvest had also resulted in a collection of around one hundred and fifty seeds from the coca fruits they had collected and these were propagated as were the seeds before them, resulting in the plantation being extended by one hundred and fifty plants. They were well away in their new venture and set off for a shopping expedition in Cairns.

The shopping list also included bags of potting mix and fertiliser which they bought from several shops to avoid any suspicion.

During the next two days, food and drink supplies were also loaded onto the trailer to take to the lease, and just as they were about to leave Cairns for the long trip back to the mining lease a call came from Nick Sabott, their Marreba contact with the Russians in Gladstone,

'Stay away from Watsonville for a couple of days, the cops are hitting it as we speak' and the call promptly ended.

Terry tried to call the number back but the message said that the number was not connected.

'Fuck,....now what?' David wanted to know.

'We just hang loose around here for another couple of days I suppose' Terry answered, 'Nothing else we can do I suppose'.

'Try calling Nick back' David suggested.

Terry pushed the redial on his phone and the line was immediately answered.

'Hang up,..I'll call you back' said the voice, presumably Nick's.

After what seemed like hours, Terry's phone rang.

'Nick?'......answered Terry.

'Some arse dobbed you pricks into the cops, I don't know who it was, my source won't say, but I'm guessing it's the prick that owns the place. The cops are destroying what they can find but they are not staying out there, give it a day and you'll be right, just watch out for the mongrel Strauss in future'. Nick then hung up.

They had arrived back at the mining lease two days after Nicks's phone call and they nervously entered the shed, other than it being unlocked and all the beer drunk and the empties left lying around the floor, you wouldn't know anyone had been there, nothing seemed to be missing?

They gingerly checked up the slope where the plantation was to find about a dozen marijuana bushes, that they had planted for their personal use, pulled from the ground and left out lying on the ground to die, but that was all, some raid they thought and shrugged.

'Let's get that prick' said David, 'And fix him for life'

'Sure, growing dope is one thing, but I think the cops might get a lot heavier with us for murder' replied Terry heading to the trailer to bring in some beer for the fridge, ' We'll just have to watch out for him, or try harder to make friends with him'.

'Fuck that, I'd rather just shoot the prick, there are so many places to hide a body around here,... he would never be found!'

● ● ● ● ● ● ● ●

Feasibility Study

The furthest Mark had been from the ACT was Sydney in New South Wales and Melbourne in Victoria, he had never ventured into Queensland even though Damo had kept at him to 'Come on up and thaw out' he had just never found time in his laid back style of life.

Mark had worked it all out on Google Maps, it was two thousand and eight hundred kilometres from his unit in Kingston in the Australian Capital Territory to Cooktown in Queensland.

Not that far when you look at it, he thought, and he knew that if he had to he could be there in three days by going hard and driving for ten hours each day, but he had decided to take all the time in the world.

Damo had told Mark that the tenure of his job was for twelve months and Mark had decided to spend at least a month to get from Canberra to Cooktown.

The western town of Dubbo was to be his first stop, it was only around four hundred kilometres, or a five hour drive, which suited him so he could become familiar with driving his cruiser, which was quite packed with gear, and towing his small caravan.

He had found a caravan park that was located almost in the heart of town and began his tutorial in setting up his van, he had meant to go 'somewhere' around Canberra to have a practice at setting it up but for some reason, or other, had never found the time, so now here at this park with an amused audience he commenced to teach himself.

It didn't take long before an elderly, and quite experienced, caravaner had sided up to him with the offer of help.

He demonstrated to Mark how to quickly get the van levelled and to connect his waste tank and water inlet and then also the power cable. He indicated towards the direction of the amenities block and mentioned that they were the filthiest he had ever seen and to make sure that Mark wore thongs in the showers there so as not to catch some horrible disease.

It was only a few minutes walk to the RSL club and Mark thought that would be the best place for dinner that evening. It wasn't, the beers were cold but the food was very ordinary and a bit canteen style which was not to his liking, so he decided to look elsewhere for future meals whilst staying there.

The next day was a look around Dubbo for a business that could install airbags to the suspension of the Landcruiser as Mark had thought the cruiser had seemed to sway a fair bit on the trip from Canberra. By late that afternoon the airbags were fitted with a gauge on the dashboard and an onboard compressor for adjustment.

Dinner that night was at the cattleman's restaurant and a very good rump steak was served, the next morning with the caravan hooked up and ready to go, today's destination being St George in Queensland which was around six hundred kilometres.

The difference that the airbags had made to the Landcruiser's suspension was quite amazing and made the vehicle feel much more stable when towing the caravan. Following one night at St George it was onto Emerald, another six hundred kilometre drive. Here the difference in temperature was very noticeable.

Travelling from Emerald to his next stop at Charters Towers and noting the signs for other cities and towns such as Townsville and Mt Isa which Mark wanted to visit but the vast distances between these towns would mean planning another trip in the future.

He had fully planned on his route to Cooktown to be through Cairns where he was planning on checking out the Great Barrier Reef and other attractions in the area, but when the signpost at Mareeba indicated Cooktown at two hundred and seventy kilometres he decided to travel straight through and bypass Cairns on this trip, plenty of time for Cairns a little later he thought.

Stopping at the Palmer River Roadhouse for fuel, Mark saw that it was also a camping ground and decided to stay over and head for Cooktown the following morning.

After reading the sign, whilst paying for his fuel, he asked the lady at the servo there for a powered site. She handed him a key to the amenities building and said,

'That's thirty five dollars, and the power is only from seven in the morning, if he gets up on time, and ten pm at night, unless it's quiet in the bar when we might shut it down early, park your caravan wherever you can find a place behind the tavern, you'll see the power posts'

He thanked the lady and took the key while still wondering what she meant about the power and it wasn't until he set up his caravan that he noticed the drone of a motor. He followed the direction of the engine noise down towards the Palmer River and discovered the 58kva generator being run by a Cat C4.4 diesel engine.

Mark had spent about two hours wandering along the Palmer River. When looking at the flow of the river he lost his bearings and turned to look at the sun starting to go towards the west yet this river was flowing towards the west, away from the coast to the east. He had just assumed that the river would have flowed towards the coast, about seventy kilometres to the east, but had discovered later that it ran to the Gulf of Carpentaria some three hundred and sixty kilometres to the west.

When checking in earlier that day Mark had noticed a paperback book for sale, 'River of Gold' written by Hector Holthouse in 1994. That afternoon Mark settled in his folding chair under the pullout canopy of his caravan and started to read his book. He was amazed at the descriptions of the savage Aboriginals attacking the miners and cannibalising the miners' dead bodies and also their horses. What an amazing story, a true story.

He had walked the few metres to the tavern at around six o'clock that evening and had ordered a chicken parmigiana for dinner which was excellent, following dinner he sat at the bar and ordered a xxx gold stubby. It wasn't long before he had entered into a conversation with a local prospector named Ivan Karabanoski who said he was camped down towards Maytown.

Ivan had described Maytown to Mark as the relic of a once thriving gold rush town.

Mark was enthralled with his stories about the town and about gold finds and, just having read the book 'River of Gold', Mark asked Ivan if there were many Aborigines around that area.

'Aborigines?...around Maytown?...Fuck no, why would you ask that? Ivan wanted to know, 'There's fuck all for them down there, no pubs or poker machines and no banks or post office to collect their dole'.

'I have just finished reading the book 'River of Gold' by Hector Holthouse and he tells of many Aborigines that were in the area back in the 1870s and that they were a real threat to the miners and that they also ate the bodies of the miners that they had killed' Mark replied.

'Yes, true, I have also read that book and, I might add, also another book that has been written about this area', I have also heard many stories of around this area, but, he added, 'You won't find many Aborigines around here these days, they all live in the towns, well most of them anyway, they enjoy the white man's way of life these days'. Ivan spoke in a well polished English voice.

He continued by saying that the modern day Aborigines now enjoy spending the money that the Government give to them and wearing the white man's clothing, drinking the white man's grog, living in the white man's housing, eating the white man's food and playing the white man's Rugby League.

Speaking of rugby league, have you noticed at the matches where *white* Aborigines are doing the so called smoking ceremony, that the real Aborinine players give them strange looks?

'The only Aborigines that whinge and bitch about the white man and the white man's Government are the 'Faux Aborigines' and you will find a lot of them in Federal Parliament, they are hard to pick out from the others as they look just like us, very rarely are these fellows black. It's not until they start talking that you can recognise them by the bullshit they speak about Land Rights and they need more money'.

Ivan went on to say, 'I mean like really, some of these blokes are a fucking joke, they stand up in parliament and say they are a 'Kalcadoon Man' or some other fucking tribe, and they are fucking whiter than me and you, for fucks sake old chap where have you been?'

'I was born and bred in Canberra, this is the first time I have ever been to Queensland, the only Aborigines that I have seen were the ones manning the 'Aboriginal Embassy' opposite the old Parliament House. Was Mark's response.

'Well,..you'll soon get used to them around these parts mate and it's not a good idea to walk around Cooktown on your own after dark and never ever, go to an ATM on your own. You'll see them in the supermarkets walking around the isles whilst having a feed of chips, or having a drink of milk, or something and discard the wrappers on the shelves so they don't have to pay at the checkout.

Generally, if they want to talk to you it's to ask you for money or smokes.....or they are offended by you and they want you to leave *their* country'. Ivan continued his summing up, 'You see, they don't have to go to work and the kids don't have to go to school, so....look, there are some good ones and I have worked with some really top Aborigines....it just seems that when they get together they don't give a fuck..and you know, when you look at it,..we would most likely be just the same if we were given everything that we needed without having to work for it'.

Mark offered, 'I spent a few years in the airforce and I must admit that I never came across any Aborigines in the armed forces, not saying that there wasn't any'.

When Ivan heard where Mark was heading he suggested a nice little caravan park in Charlotte Street he might like and it was only a short walk to town, and, make sure you check out the museum, some good local history in there'.

Mark had thanked Ivan for the good company and conversation and had said goodnight as he headed to his caravan. He had not quite made it there when suddenly the hum of the Cat diesel stopped and the place was plunged into darkness, and it *was* dark.

It was so dark, and as it happened Mark remembered turning around, he now slowly made a half turn back again, hoping that he was back on the course that he was when the lights went off.

He placed his right arm out in front of him and slowly walked forward, it was very eerie as he could not see anything at all.

He was thinking that surely someone around here would have had some sort of light on, but there was nothing but blackness when suddenly his hand touched something metallic at about the same time that his legs also touched something metallic and he fell forward striking his head on the bullbar of his Landcruiser.

He finally found the door to his caravan and flicked on the 12v LED light and sat down at the little table, he took his telephone out of his pocket and looked at it stupidly, it has a torch and he didn't even think of it. He turned on the camera of his phone and reversed it so that he could check out the condition of his head, it was quite bruised and would look even worse in the morning he surmised.

He had a great breakfast at the bistro the next morning, then he headed towards Cooktown which was about one hundred and ten kilometres.

He was in no hurry and stopped at Lakeland, a small town with a population of three hundred people and after wondering about the town for an hour had discovered the local history of Lakeland that went back to 1877. Over time the larger properties had been divided into many smaller farms and the largest surviving property of 140,000 acres, which was within Mark's selection criteria, was bought by the Queensland Government in 2016 and added to the states protected area network. Sadly, Mark had ruled out any activity in this area for the magnitude that JCE was interested in.

He found the small caravan park in Charlotte Street Cooktown that Ivan had told him about and had booked onto a powered site for two weeks. A perfect place for a base he had thought. Besides a visit to the museum, Ivan had also recommended both the RSL and the Bowling club for meals, both around a one and a half kilometre walk.

During his walking down to the clubs and the time that he had spent there he was starting to doubt Ivan Karabanoski's advice with respect to Aborigines, the people he had seen so far were quite friendly and only a few of them had asked him for money.

He was on his way back to the caravan park at about eight o'clock when he was asked by an elderly Aborigine if he could spare two dollars, as Mark was looking for change in his pocket he was struck from behind with great force, something had hit him in the centre of his back and had taken the wind from his lungs and before he could turn around he was struck again.

It was just after eleven o'clock pm when Mark opened his eyes and saw the dim light gleaming down on him. It was the light that was mounted on the power pole that was three metres to his right. He had no idea where he was, he sat up from the strip of grass that he was lying on, it hurt, his back was very painful just above his buttocks. He looked across at the building in front of him and could just make out in the feeble light that it was the Post Office.

Unable to stand, he crawled towards the Post Office and used the white timber railing in front of the building to pull himself to his feet. As he got to his feet he remembered the great pain he suffered in his back whilst talking to the Aborigine, he checked for his wallet, but it was gone! His car keys were also gone.

It took a while for him to realise what had happened as he slowly began to walk towards the caravan park, each step brought pain to the area around his kidneys but he finally made it to the park and his caravan and he saw that his Landcruiser was not there.

'Fuck it….no'! He called out to no one, and as he went to open the caravan's door, he then realised that he did not have the key to his caravan and was locked out. Placing his hands on each side of his head he slumped to the ground, the pain shot up his back and he again passed out.

It was daylight when he opened his eyes and he realised that he was lying on the ground looking towards the driveway that exited the caravan park as his memory slowly came back.

He sat up and the pain in his back also reminded him of last night's events, remembering that his Landcruiser was missing he quickly looked around and saw the caravan but the Landcruiser was not there.

Slowly getting to his feet amid the pain around his kidneys, he also remembered that he had no key to enter his caravan.

Stumbling up to the caravan he gently lowered himself to the ground and crawled underneath the caravan to where the water tank is installed, reaching up the the chassis cross rail above the water tank he retrieved the magnetic key holder, which also had a safety chain attached, and removed the two keys, that were connected with a keyring, inside the holder.

Mark had finally got inside his caravan and he lay on the bed and again passed out.

It was almost three o'clock in the afternoon when he had again awoken and the memory flooded back to him as he slowly got from the bed. The back pain had subsided somewhat and he was able to walk a lot easier as he contemplated his next move.

'The Police' he exclaimed to himself as he opened the caravan door to yet again confirm that his Landcruiser was not there.

'What time was it when you left the RSL club?' The senior constable of a force of ten stationed at Cooktown was asking Mark.

• • • • • • • •

Senior Constable Jason Walsh was on his second posting since graduating from the police academy in Oxley, Brisbane. His first posting had been Townsville where he had served for three years and he had just been promoted to Senior Constable after serving in Cooktown for two years.

Jason Walsh was born in Queanbeyan New South Wales, just south of the Australian Capital Territory.

Jason was a sole child and his parents were both public servants and both worked for the Department of Supply at the offices in Constitution Avenue in Canberra.

The family home was in Cameron Road, just down from the Queanbeyan South Public School which Jason had attended, then later schooling at Karrabar High School which was just one block away from the primary school.

Following attaining the HSC Jason left school and decided to join the army, it was a spur of the moment thing as his best friend from high school was also joining the army, but it had been his friend's lifetime wish. His parents had tried to talk him out of it but to no avail.

Jason joined the 1st Recruit Training Battalion and was sent to do his training at Kapooka, his school friend failed his medical and was refused entry to the army.

It was a whole new experience for Jason, he had never taken communal showers and slept in a barrack with other males, nor had he ever had to queue for his meals and be denied a selection of foods.

He thoroughly enjoyed the rigorous training and the training with weapons but found the unarmed combat training to be a bit too tough for him as it was something that he had avoided all his life, he was the sort of person to avoid confrontation at all costs, most likely from his bringing up and being an only child with no siblings to play and fight with.

On his third night of sleeping in the barrack, someone had shorted his bed sheet which had upset Jason greatly and made him feel that the rest of the platoon was ganging up on him.

Another recruit named Les Morton, who was part Aboriginal, had befriended Jason and had told him,

'It was that arshole Bryan Bennet who did that bed thing to you, do you want some help to get back at the prick?'

'Do you mean, do the same to him?' Jason had responded.

'Fuck no! That won't work, he'll only do it to some other poor prick, no, we'll fix the bastard properly, OK?'

Jason had no idea what Les had meant but he agreed to go along with him.

The next day after training he accompanied Les to the kitchen at the mess where Les asked the 'dishie' for a small freezer bag.

They then went towards the training area in the bush and Les found a 'bull' ant nest, then taking a small stick he placed it on the nest, and the stick immediately became covered in ants. Les then picked up the stick and quickly placed it inside the small freezer bag and tied the opening.

'This'll fix that fucking Bryan, fucking Bennet' Les said laughing in anticipation.

'He'll know its me' said Jason nervously.

'So what? Just stand up the prick, you're not frightened of him,....are you?'

'He's a pretty big bloke, and he does well in the unarmed combat training' said Jason.

'Well..bro, you need to learn to stand up for yourself, generally, big blokes like Bennet are all piss and wind, you know..they are all bluff, once you stand up to pricks like him they usually back down pretty quick', Les went on to give Jason some confidence, 'If he has a go at you, then you need to get in the first hit, but..after you hit him, don't just stand there looking to see what effect it had, you need to hit him again and keep hitting him until he either backs off or, goes down..got it?'

'He'll fucking kill me' Jason was really getting worried now.

'Kill you! Fucking bullshit, you can sort that dude out bro, believe me, anyway, if it goes wrong I'll be there to administer first aid. Nar only joking, you can clean him up, no sweat.

The scream that night, just after lights out, was indescribable, Bennet had lept from his bed brushing ants from him as he cried out with each ant bite. Then he looked straight across at Jason.

'Walsh....you fucking prick...you did this, your fucked' said Bennet as he started to approach Jason.

Without answering Jason walked towards Bennet and Bennet stopped, it would seem that he didn't expect Jason to approach him. Jason came up to Bennet and hit him fully in his face as hard as he could, Bennet fell to the floor unconscious.

Bennet was transferred to the Kapooka Hospital and Jason was charged by the military police with assault and discharged from the army. Les had said, sorry brother, to Jason and added that he had no idea there would be such consequences.

Jason was pretty pissed off but did not hold a grudge against Les, Les in return gave Jason his home address in Townsville, Queensland, and told him to keep in contact.

Jason did not want to return to Queanbeyan and thought he would check out Les's hometown Townsville.

He fell in love with Townsville, the weather was just perfect and the people were friendly.

He found a job at the 'Purple Pub' on The Strand, as a cellar man and quite enjoyed it. He also discovered that the job also gave him plenty of opportunities to practice his new found pugilistic skills, much to the satisfaction of his employer.

It didn't take Jason long to earn a reputation for his ability to quell fights and clear bars and he was in demand around town as a bouncer at many events.

It was actually a somewhat drunk, off duty local police sergeant, that he had bounced one night at a function that he later became friends with, who talked him into joining the Queensland Police Force. The rest was history!

Mark's case was like a breath of fresh air to Jason as the only cases that he had been involved in since being in Cooktown had been domestic violence which seemed so repetitive and quite often, the same faces. It was for this reason that he had applied for a transfer to the Highway Patrol which now had two full time officers in Cooktown.

● ● ● ● ● ● ● ●

'About eight,..eight thirty' Mark replied and grimaced in pain.

'Mate, I think that it might be best if I run you around to the hospital and get them to check you out before we get into the full details' Jason said as he stood up from the front desk and told the other constable to watch the fort for a while.

There was no waiting at the hospital, it seemed that Constable Jason was quite popular there with the doctors and staff, Mark was ushered into the triage room almost straight away once they had his details and his Medicare card number.

The check revealed severe bruising around his upper torso and lower back but nothing that would not heal within a week or so with the aid of some Panadol Forte pain killers which they gave to Mark. Mark accompanied the senior constable back to the police station where Mark completed his statement and report.

The constable then offered Mark a lift back to the caravan park but Mark had declined the offer and suggested that a walk may be helpful in the healing process.

Upon arrival at his caravan, Mark used his MacBook Air to cancel the two credit cards that had been in his wallet and his insurance company to notify them about his car. He then went to the hiding place he had in the Caravan and checked that he still had the ten thousand dollars cash that he had stored there and placed one thousand in his back pocket. He felt a bit naked without his wallet, it was now six thirty and Mark headed to the RSL Club for his first meal of the day. He would call Father Damien with the news later that evening.

As soon as Mark had walked into the club he recognised the old Aboriginal that had asked him for money last night and he didn't hesitate and walked up to where he was sitting with a group of other Aborigines

'Hey you black prick' Mark called out to him, 'Are these your accomplices from last night'? he said indicating to the other's at the table.

'Ay don't know whut you are talkin bout brother' he replied.

None of the other people at the table looked up but Mark noticed that there were quite a few empty stubbies, as well as full stubbies, on the table.

'You don't seem to need a couple of dollars tonight though?' Mark said as he walked away from the table and went to the bar to order a meal.

'Hey!...feeling better'? It was the constable, Jason who was standing at the bar, now wearing civvy clothes, just about to order a drink, 'Can I get you a beer'?

'Thanks, Jason, a xxxx gold stubbie will be nice' Mark agreed.

'Y'reckon that's your man?' Said Jason nodding towards the old bloke.

'That's the one that asked for the money before I got hit, it wasn't him that hit me, it must have been one of the younger blokes sitting at the table' Mark replied

'They all know that there is not a thing we can do about it, it's pretty sad but you didn't get to see who hit you, you can't identify any those clowns sitting there,..can you?'

Mark agreed that he only really suspected that the person, or persons, who hit him were there at the table, as he didn't see who it was and it seemed a coincidence that they seem to have money to spend tonight.

'Are you eating here tonight?' asked Jason, 'I often have a steak here during the week'

They both ate their steaks at the bar and drank a few stubbies, Jason asked Mark if he would like to get even with the brothers later tonight, he told him that it wouldn't get his wallet or car back, but it would make him feel better.

'These blokes are usually the last ones to leave the club, especially when they are cashed up, and they will buy take away's, and it would seem that they are cashed up, and I just happen to have some Covid masks at my house just up the road along with a couple of six hundred millimetre lengths of one inch HD poly pipe, Jason went on, 'So,...if you are keen we will leave just on closing and don the masks and the poly pipe, what do you reckon Mark? Might find out where your truck is'.

'I'm in Jason,..fucking oath mate, I hope you're for real?'

Jason responded by holding his hand out to shake and said that no one is to know and that *is* important and to try not to kill any of them as it might get complicated. Mark shook his hand and said,

'Just say when mate!' Mark did not hesitate to shake Jason's hand and ordered two more beers.

They left the RSL just before ten o'clock as the barman called for 'Last Drinks' and walked over the road and up the hill for about two hundred and fifty metres to Jason's Qld Police residence.

'Come on in Mark', Jason called whilst opening the front door, 'You don't have to be quiet, there is no one else living here except me, my wife couldn't handle Cooktown and moved back to Brisbane and lives with her mum. Here, grab this' Jason said handing a piece of poly pipe to Mark and then he opened a drawer and took out two face covid masks.

They went back towards the club and stood in the shadows on the opposite side of the road. They did not have to wait very long before the Aborigines came out of the front door carrying two cartons of beer in cans.

There were seven males, including the old man, and two females, Jason told Mark to watch out for the

'Ginns' as they would most likely attack them, but a whack on the backs of their legs with the poly would generally change their minds.

The group moved from the entrance of the club and headed towards the river where they settled at a park picnic table, Jason and Mark were following behind them in the shadows and Jason said to Mark,

'Not too hard Mark and don't hit any of them in the face or head, just around the shoulders is the best, we can't kill any of them remember, and leave the old bloke alone for questioning, don't hit him'.

They advanced up to the group rapidly, they had a radio playing 'Life Goes On' by Ed Sheeran, it was very loud and the group did not hear their attackers until almost half of them had been struck and were on the ground. Contrary to what Jason had said about the Ginns, they just grabbed one carton of beer and ran away screaming.

It hadn't taken long to put them all on the ground and Mark just knew that he had broken ribs on at least two of them.

They lay on the ground in submission and begging for mercy and Jason said to the old fella,

'Where's that white fella's wallet bro?' As he jabbed him in the ribs with the poly pipe.

'Dow know what you mean boss'.

Another, much harder jab in the old fella's ribs and this time he screamed out,

'He's in the river boss, with all dem cards too, we only tookem money boss'

'And where is the white fella's truck' asked Jason giving the old fella a very hard jab in the ribs making him suck air which made it impossible for him to answer straight away. Jason asked him the same question again, but this time he used his poly pipe to hit the nearest man to the old fella across his shoulders making him scream out in pain. The old fella said,

'Fella in Hopevale buy him boss'

'Which fella in Hopevale?' And Jason gave the nearest man another whack.

'The fella Goodwin, Thomas, yeah he's the Thomas Goodwin, he buy him boss, too right boss'.

'If I find that you fella's are telling me the bullshit I'll fucking kill the lot of you and burn your fucking homes'.

Having said that, Jason indicated to Mark that it was time to go and they disappeared over the road into the darkness.

Mark handed a cold tinny (can of beer) to Jason from one of the two six packs he had taken from the Aborigines. They walked back to Jason's house and drank the rest of them as they talked about investigating this man at Hopevale called Thomas Goodwin, Jason said that he would check out the name on police files and they would go and talk to him tomorrow afternoon at Hopevale. They both agreed that it had been a great night and Jason had told Mark that he would pick him up tomorrow afternoon at about two o'clock, and added,

'For fucks sake, don't breath a word of this to anyone'.

Mark walked back to the caravan park feeling much better following the bit of exercise he had performed with his new mate Jason.

The next morning Mark had made a call to Father Damien's home and was lucky to catch him, as he was about to leave for his office. He told Damo what had happened but had omitted the interviewing of the old Aboriginal man last night.

He had told Damo about Jason and how helpful he had been and that he had contacted the banks about his cards and said that the insurance company would not do anything about his car for a while until the police found it, but they had offered him a hire car for use in the interim.

Father Damien suggested that Mark move down to Cairns to get everything sorted, he could collect his cards from the respective banks and put pressure on the insurance company in person, 'That always works' insisted Father Damien, 'And you can collect your new vehicle in Cairns, doubt there would be any dealers in Cooktown'.

Mark agreed that would be the best bet, he would leave his caravan at the caravan park and find a short term unit rental in Cairns.

At exactly one thirty that afternoon Jason arrived at the caravan park in his police Landcruiser and found Mark and gave him one of his police shirts to put on for the afternoon to avoid any one that they would talk to today becoming suspicious of Mark, they would assume him to be just another copper.

Jason had an address for a Thomas Goodwin at Hopevale and they were on their way to pay him a visit.

It is close to fifty kilometres from Cooktown to Hopevale, on the way there Jason asked Mark what it was that brought him to Cooktown and Mark had told Jason about the feasibility study that he was conducting for a business conglomerate.

'So you are buying up cattle properties around the area?' Jason asked

'Maybe, it just depends on what size the properties are and their carrying capacity and, of course, what price the property will be available at. There are a lot of variables involved and it is still early days, but this sort of shit, losing my car, will set me back a bit'. Mark also went on to tell Jason of his plan to move down to Cairns until he can get another vehicle.

Hopevale is an Aboriginal Shire and has alcohol restrictions of 1 x carton of 30 cans of 375ml beer, a total of 11.25 litres of beer or one bottle of 750ml unfortified wine, per person on foot or per car and per boat, regardless of how many people are in the vehicle.

This means, as there are no liquor stores in Hopevale and the nearest is at Cooktown, then to bring alcohol into town by vehicle means only one carton of beer per trip.

This restriction is for all public and private areas, one of the reasons so many of them frequent Cooktown.

They found the address that they were looking for and a pregnant woman inside the house with two young children claimed that she had not seen or heard from her husband, Thomas Goodwin, for about six days but believed he was in Weipa visiting relatives. Other random interviews with people around Hopevale came up with similar stories, or some just did not know him, but, knew of him.

A description of the missing vehicle had gone Australia wide and, as Jason said, 'It would be only a matter of time'.

It was four days after the Landcruiser had been stolen when a truck driver returning from Weipa had noticed a reflection that was well off the road in the bush on the Northern side of the small township of Coen. He had decided to investigate and saw skid marks on the bend in the road heading into the scrub, he had followed the skid marks for about twelve metres and came across an Isuzu Pantech Truck, the truck was upside down with a body trapped inside the cab. Inside the Pantech, was a Landcruiser utility. It wasn't Marks Landcruiser, it was, however, another stolen late model Landcruiser that had been reported missing from The Archer River Roadhouse some two weeks previous.

Mark had taken the Dash 8 air service from Cooktown to Cairns and had found temporary accommodation in the form of a three bedroom, three bathroom, unit in Digger Street, just a short walk from the city.

His motor vehicle insurance company had told him that if the vehicle was not recovered within twenty one days then it would be written off, if it was recovered after that period, then it became the property of the insurance company to dispose of it as they wished. It looked like a two, to three week stay in Cairns for Mark, plus the time to get a new vehicle organised.

It was a good time to research what he could with respect to rural properties as described in his brief from JCE.

Cooktown was to be considered the most northern geographical cut off point for rural properties for the purpose of transportation.

The property area is required to carry a minimum of 50,000 head of cattle with a forecast production of 25,000 bullocks per annum after 2 years with a target of 750kg live weight per head, or approximately 18,000 tonnes.

With the aid of data made available from The Queensland Government Department of Resources, he was able to make a list of properties in the area west of Cooktown and obtain an indicative land valuation as per the Valuer General where possible. With this list, he was able to link properties until the required carrying capacity was achieved and then calculate his budgeted property value of ten million dollars against the possible combinations of indicative value. It was not going to be easy, especially when it came to approaching the landowners.

As the residing Police Constable from Laura, being the closest station to the fatal accident of the truck rollover, was away attending court, Senior Constable Walsh, was assigned the task of investigating the accident and submitting a report to the coroner. The forensic traffic police had attended the scene and had forwarded their findings on the fatality to Jason.

Jason discovered that the deceased man was the owner of the Isuzu Pantech truck that was involved in the single vehicle accident and had collected the vehicle that was being transported in the back of the Pantech from an address in Weipa. The address of the collection point was sent to the Weipa Police Station and was confirmed to be the parking area on John Evens Drive at the Weipa Airport.

The deceased man's address was found, via the trucks registration details, to be a Manunda address in Cairns.

Jason had contacted the Cairns Police to visit the man's home and interview the man's wife or partner.

The Cains Police had to reject the request due to staffing shortages caused by sickness, the Cooktown Officer in Charge directed Senior Constable Walsh to transfer to the Cairns Police Station on a temporary basis to enable him to conduct his investigation into the deceased truck driver and the stolen vehicle and to investigate if the vehicle stolen in Cooktown was in any way connected.

Jason had contacted Mark in Cairns and had told him that he was coming down to Cairns for about a week and that they should catch up,

'Where are you staying?' Mark asked

'Haven't found anywhere yet, most likely the Colonial Club is where they recommend' Jason Replied.

'Well I'm staying in Digger Street and I have two spare bedrooms and bathrooms if you want to go halves?'

'Done' was Jason's reply, 'I should be there about three pm and I'll have to report to the operations officer in charge and I can meet you at around four thirty. What do you reckon, a few beers and a feed at the 'Rattle n Hum'?'

It didn't seem to take more than ten minutes to walk from Digger Steet to the Esplanade where 'Rattle n Hum' are located, the beers were cold and at a good price and the food was just excellent.

'So,..you haven't told me why you are in Cairns' Mark asked

'I'm here on business, investigating a fatal accident that happened on the Peninsula Development Road near Coen. A truck ran off the road into the bush and killed the driver.'

'You have to come to Cairns to investigate a prang?' Mark queried.

'There is a bit more to it, there was a stolen 78 series Cruiser on the back of the truck that was, presumably, heading to Cairns......' Mark interrupted him.

'My truck...?'

'No, sadly, Mark, it wasn't. But it was another Cruiser about the same as yours but this one was a single cab' Jason explained, 'And I am checking to see if they, the vehicle thefts, might be linked, the Cairns coppers are short on staff so I have a transfer down here to investigate. I'm in the boss's unmarked car and I'll work in plain clothes'.

Following dinner, it was a stroll to the Reef Casino, a few more beers, and a hopeless game of blackjack, then back to the unit at around one thirty that next morning.

It was a late start the next morning with a walk down to 'La Pizza' on the Esplanade for breakfast, Jason left Mark at the restaurant and went back to the unit to get his car, Mark went down to Woolies to get a couple of things.

Jason had found the address and a talk with the occupant of that address had confirmed that her partner had received a call from someone to collect the car from Weipa and drop it off at an address in Portsmith, she wasn't sure where it was but her partner had often picked up cars and taken them to this address where the cars were put onto B Doubles that were returning empty to either Brisbane or Sydney. That is all she could tell Jason.

It was after four hours of sitting at a desk and making telephone calls to local Cairns transport companies and asking about empty B Doubles transporting vehicles down to either Brisbane, Sydney or Melbourne, that one company receptionist mentioned that a really nice looking 'red' Landcruiser was put onto Steve Brown's B Double truck just last week to be taken to Melbourne,

'I assume the Landcruiser was going to Melbourne as that's where Brownie's next pickup was'.

'When will Brownie be back in the depot?' Jason casually asked.

'Actually,...Hmm,..tomorrow,...tomorrow morning at around five am' the lady said.

'How would I recognise him?' Jason wanted to know.

'You don't have to be here at that time, I'll see him at about nine o'clock, and I can tell him to contact you if you like?'

'No...no, that won't be necessary, I would rather you didn't say anything about this call please, not to anyone'. Jason added quickly.

'I hope I haven't gotten anybody into trouble' she said resentfully. 'Brownie drives a green Western Star with the name Brown Transport written on each door'.

'I assure you, you have not got anyone into trouble, please don't speak about this conversation, goodbye…and thank you'.

Jason hung up the telephone, 'Can't be right' he thought out loud, 'Too fucking easy, much too easy'.

'What do you reckon Jase, we have dinner at the Casino tonight?' Suggested Mark just after Jason had got in and was on his second beer. Jason had declined the offer telling Mark that he had to be gone at around four in the morning and then he told him a little about the day's activities, but he omitted the part about the 'red' Landcruiser.

The boys enjoyed A quiet night that night, if you can call a quiet night a full carton of xxxx Gold Stubbies and half a bottle of Makers Mark Whiskey with two delivery Pizza Hut pizzas.

Well, it was Friday and there were two games of NRL on the TV that night.

Jason, with fellow Police Officer Constable Neal Hardy from the Cairns Police CID, had arrived at Fearnley Street, Portsmith, at just after four o'clock, there were three B Double trucks pulled up just before the transport company gates that were still closed.

Jason slowly drove past the trucks and saw that the last truck had the name Brown Transport displayed on the door.

It was still dark as Jason parked the car behind the last truck,

'You go to the passenger side and I'll go to the driver's side', Jason commanded, 'He may be asleep, but if the passenger door is unlocked then open it and I'll do the same with the drivers side door, just play it by ear'.

The man was not asleep, but looking at his phone as Jason opened his door and showed the man his badge. The expression on the man's face was that of pure shock, it changed to worse when the passenger door was flung open by another person showing a police badge.

'Relax….relax,….just want to ask you some questions' said Jason with his hand resting on his holstered Glock.

'What the fucking….hell!' The truck driver was lost for words in his sudden shock.

'We just need to ask you some questions, now please step down from the truck….please' said Jason with his hand still on his Glock.

'Fuck you,..get off my truck, fucking arseholes' as the truck driver attempted to push Jason away from him through the driver's side door.

'OK, have it your way' said Jason quickly as he grabbed the man's arm whilst jumping backwards off the step tank of the Western Star truck, bringing the driver falling after him and landing on his back on the ground beside the truck, meanwhile Jasons colleague had got down from the passenger side door and was already at the drivers side when the driver had landed on the ground. The constable went straight down with his knee landing on the driver's throat as Jason started to put handcuffs on his wrists. Following a brief struggle with lots of shouting from the truck driver, the truck driver was sitting on the ground with his hands cuffed behind his back.

The driver's shouts had brought the drivers from the two trucks parked in front of the Browns Transport truck.

'What the fucks going on here then?' called one of the drivers.

Jason held up his badge and said 'Police,...stay back there!' As his colleague was starting to put the driver into the back of the police car.

'Leave the poor bastard alone fuck yers, what's he done?' The other truck driver called.

'Just mind your own business and stay back there' Jason repeated to the other truck drivers.

The handcuffs had been removed and Steve Brown had been placed in a small interview room that contained only one small table and three chairs. He had briefed the interviewers, Detective Sergeant Rohan Scott and Detective Senior Constable Howard Fergusson on the case and the events leading up to detaining Steve Brown. Within two and a half hours the interviewers had the names of the stolen vehicle receivers in Melbourne and had learnt of their spare parts operation.

The Victorian Police, Melbourne CID had been advised of the events that were discovered in Cairns and within twenty four hours they had exposed a major stolen vehicle operation that was receiving vehicles from all Australian states and turning them into spare parts for the busy Australian vehicle spare parts market.

The information pertaining to the Cairns incident was that the Melbourne car theft operation's Far North Queensland's operative was a male suspect named Antonio Calabishi.

He was known to offer indigenous people in remote areas, ten thousand dollars cash, for late model four wheel drive vehicles with no questions asked. The man Antonio Calabishi was the deceased Isuzu Pantech truck driver in the accident near Coen last week.

Jason remained in Cairns for the next three days completing his report on Steve Brown and appearing at the formal charging and remanding in custody of the offender. Jason had said to Steve Brown that had he just got down from the truck in a nice manner, then he would most likely have been granted bail, his aggression had not done him any favours.

Mark had already been looking for a replacement vehicle and had found one on 'carsales.com' located in Brisbane, it was a similar vehicle to the one he had lost, including some of the accessories.

Mark had contacted Father Damien and had asked for an advance of one hundred thousand dollars to pay for the replacement vehicle, he could repay Father Damien once the insurance company had compensated Mark, if necessary.

The money was in Mark's bank account the next day and Mark made arrangements to fly to Brisbane to collect his new ute.

The seller of the 78 series Landcruiser had collected Mark from the airport and had driven him to his home in Brisbane North where the vehicle was garaged. Mark was beside himself once he saw the condition of the 'Midnight Blue' coloured car, it was immaculate with a matching coloured metal canopy, it had a polished stainless steel nudge bar, an adjustable, front and rear, high lift kit, front and rear diff lockers, rear airbags with internal air pressure gauges and onboard compressor, a four tonne capacity electric winch and was fitted with Recaro leather seats.

The only thing it needed was a towbar, which Mark had organised to be fitted on his way back to Cooktown at Redcliffe in Brisbane North.

It was almost seven o'clock when Mark returned to the caravan park at Cooktown and he had decided on a steak at the RSL for dinner that evening, on his way to the club he walked across the road to Jason's house, he found Jason sitting on his front verandah with a stubby in his hand.

'Well, fuck me, your back, I'll get you a stubby, have a seat'.

Mark sat down and asked   Jason if he wanted to go to the RSL for dinner.

'Mate!..I was given a whole rump today by the sarge and I was just about to slice a steak off it for a feed, why not stay here and have a steak with me, I'm nearly out of piss though if you wouldn't mind grabbing a slab from the pub while I get the steaks cut?'

'You're on' said Mark as he headed across the road to the Sovereign Hotel's bottle shop.

After dinner and a few stubby's, Jason was telling Mark about the investigation in Cairns,

'It seems that the Pantech truck driver from Cairns, Antonio Calabishi, had put the word out to the Abbo's that he would pay ten grand cash for late model Landcruiser's and it's a good bet that our friend, Thomas Goodwin from Hopevale, has ten grand in his pocket.

Watsonville Station

Mark Crompton had left Cooktown and was towing his caravan on his way to meet the station owners that he had been in contact with by telephone with a view to the purchase of the property, he had made arrangements with them to camp in his caravan on the stations for the duration of his visit to allow him time to look over the properties.

It had taken him a little over four weeks to inspect five properties that may have fallen within JCE's criteria but sadly none of them did, mainly it was the price wanted by the owners of the properties that eliminated them.

Even though the price of some of the stations was within the criteria, the beef carrying capacity was not and the property would need to be linked to another property, but the then combined price of the properties would exceed the JCE criteria.

There was but one property in the district left that Mark had yet to visit due to the fact that he had been unable to contact them, so he had left that property until last and now was the time.

He had tried calling the telephone number that he had, but to no avail, so he decided to make an unannounced visit.

He had left Laura on Palmervale Road and then turned onto Kiamba Road, after travelling for just over five hours his odometer showed he had travelled three hundred and thirty kilometres, he estimated that he still had approximately forty kilometres until he would reach the homestead of Watsonville Station, it was five fifty in the afternoon when he saw a turnoff to his right and decided to turn onto it and find a place to camp for the night, he had proceeded all of thirty metres along this track and was pulling off to the right hand side of the track where there was room beside the track for a campsite, the vehicle was almost stationary and suddenly his steering wheel spun to the left knocking his hand from the steering wheel, he simultaneously heard a loud bang.

Mark had completely stopped the car once this happened and got out to look at what might have caused this, walking from the driver's side door and around the front of the vehicle he immediately saw that the left hand side front tyre was completely flat.

Whilst bending down for a closer examination of the tyre Mark noticed what seemed to be a metal spike protruding from the centre of the track, then looking closer at the spike he saw other spikes that were almost completely across the track.

Luckily for him as he had almost stopped the vehicle to turn right, the right hand wheel had just missed one of the spikes in the track but the left hand wheel had struck another, it was fortunate that he had completely stopped otherwise all four tyres on the Landcruiser and the two tyres on the caravan could have been spiked.

Leaving the Landcruiser exactly where Mark had stopped it, in the centre of the track he commenced to jack up the front left side of the vehicle, as the wheel came clear of the track it exposed the metal spike that had penetrated the tyre.

Mark removed the wheel and then realised that he could not put on one of his two spare wheels until he removed that spike from the ground, grabbing the spike with his hands he realised that it was firmly in the ground and using a hammer started to strike at the spike to loosen it in the ground surrounding it.

The spike did not move with a hammer blow but rather it repelled the hammer with each blow,

Strange thought Mark, they must be driven in very deep. He then took the small maddock-type pick that he had bought for prospecting and attempted to dig out the spike.

Whilst digging around the spike with the hope of loosening it, he struck something else that felt and sounded like metal, beside the spike on the side towards the other spikes, he then realised that the spikes seemed to be connected together with a metal bar, or something, under the ground.

Giving up his attempt to dig the ground around the spike, he took a beer from the caravan's fridge and sat down in front of the Landcruiser, drinking his beer and staring intently at the spike. Finishing his beer, he then fitted the spare wheel to the front of the Landcruiser and then jacked the front up higher.

Looking around Mark found two large rocks that were just a bit higher than the spike and placed one rock on each side of the spike, he then carefully lowered the jack so that the left hand wheel now sat on top of the rocks that were either side of the spike.

Moving the Landcruiser very slowly backward away from the spikes, Mark then reversed the caravan off the track and stopped just adjacent to the spikes and decided to camp there for the night.

The next morning whilst surveying the track section that had the spikes, it became obvious to Mark that where he had reversed the caravan into and spent the night, was in fact, a by-pass for the section of the track containing the spikes.

'Well fuck me' Mark said aloud to no one and then prepared some breakfast.

He had just begun to eat his breakfast of toast and coffee when he heard the sound of a vehicle in the distance, he guessed it was on the Kiamba Road as it got louder and closer to the track that he had turned onto and he assumed that it would go past him. The vehicle, however, slowed and turned onto the track where Mark was parked.

David Barnes and Terry Andrews both got quite a shock seeing a caravan and Landcruiser ute parked in their by-pass on the track leading to their lease and they had to stop to avoid the spikes that they had installed to keep out unwanted visitors.

Mark Jumped up from sitting on the caravan steps with both arms in the air about to scream out 'STOP!' But the vehicle had already stopped in the middle of the track just in front of the spikes.

'Doing a bit of camping mate?' Asked David while getting from the Nissan driver's side.

'You just stopped in time mate! there's spikes in the road there' said Mark pointing to the track with the visible spikes.

Before David could reply, Terry said 'Yeah, it's the pricks that own the property, they're trying to keep people out for some reason or other, they're a fucking nuisance'.

'I'm Barnsy Mate, this is Terry', said David holding out his hand towards Mark', 'We've got a mining lease up the road here'.

'The spikes are a real prick, they caught us out when we first arrived', lied Terry, 'We dug the fuckers up but Stan put them back in, so we just drive around the pricks now, just where you're camped is our detour actually'.

'What brings you out here?' Asked David.

'I'm on my way to see the owners of Watsonville' replied Mark.

'Well they mustn't know you're coming' interjected Terry, 'Cos they're on their way to Chillagoe, we passed em earlier, and they usually stay overnight'

'Well, I haven't been able to get them on the phone so I thought I would just call out there'.

'It must be important, travelling all that way on the spec of meeting up with them?' Terry was wondering why this bloke would be looking for Stan Straus and David Watson. 'You can camp up at the lease with us if you want, it's only about twenty four Kays up the road'.

Mark appreciated the offer and thought why not, more county to see and he would have to camp somewhere tonight.

Terry said to move his rig forward so that they could get past with the Nissan and then to follow.

The three of them were enjoying a beer at the mining lease, Mark had noticed a few Marijuana plants growing amongst the Coca bushes but he didn't recognise the bushes as Coca, like most people wouldn't.

'Do you mine much gold?' Mark asked.

'Fuck all' said David, not thinking.

'We get enough to get by on and a little extra' Terry quickly put in, 'we also do a bit of detecting around other parts of the river and get some good nuggets from time to time, at around three grand an ounce you can get a good days pay on some days'.

'Wow!' Whistled Mark, 'I didn't realise that gold was that price these days'.

'The next morning as Mark was getting ready to leave, Terry had told him that the owners wouldn't be back at the station till the afternoon and that he and Barnsy were going fishing at a good spot that was on the way to Watsonville if he wanted to join them and they would have a feed of Barra for lunch.

'Sounds good!' answered Mark, 'I really do appreciate you guys thanks'.

It was a top spot on the river that Terry and Dave had shown Mark. The fishing was excellent, they asked Mark to keep it to himself, and then laughed,

'As if' said Barnsy, 'Those pricks would shoot anyone they saw fishing just here, it's their favourite spot too,' meaning the Watsonville owners.

Barnsy had a disk from a plough that he used as a hotplate and they cooked barramundi and drank beers beside the river, it was a great afternoon.

Terry told Mark to keep in touch as he was preparing to leave for Watsonville, he also told Mark that they would be leaving for Mareeba the next morning to collect some gear and then he gave him his Iridium satellite phone number and said to give him a call next time he's out here.

It was three o'clock when Mark had arrived at Watsonville, it was not what he was expecting. Compared to the properties that Mark had been inspecting during the last few weeks Watsonville looked like a dump, to put it mildly.

His car had been surrounded by barking dogs as soon as he had driven into the driveway, more of a track, to the house, which looked like more of a shed than a house. He waited in the car to see if anyone would come from the house out to him.

It was not long before a man emerged from the door at the front of the house and yelled at the dogs to 'Get Back', he then walked up to Mark, as Mark would down his window.

'Are you lost and blind?' Asked Stan Strauss.

'No, not lost, I am looking for the owner of Watsonville' Mark answered the man who looked very upset to see someone in his driveway.

'Well this is private property, you have driven past about a dozen signs telling you that, so why are you here?'

'To see the owner of the property, is that You?' Mark tried again.

'Your trespassing' said the man, 'And you must be fucking blind because you would have driven past a dozen signs that say No Trespassing!'

Mark saw that this was going nowhere and as Terry had told him that 'This bloke was a total fuckwit and not to let him put it over him', remembering these words Mark said to the man,

'What are you? A fucking idiot or just fucking deaf. Can you not hear that I am here to see the owner'. Mark could see the man did not look so confident when he spoke to him in this tone.

'Are you police?' Asked the man.

'Do I look like a fucking copper? doe's this look like a fucking police car? for fucks sake, are you the owner!' Asked Mark becoming agitated.

'Are you from the Government?' The man now wanted to know.

'Mate, whoever you are, I am just a private person with a proposition for the owner, or owner's of this property, if you don't want to hear me then just say so without all of this fucking around and I will gladly go because I do not need this sort of bullshit'.

'Yud, better come inside then', the man said to Mark as he slowly walked back to the wide open house door.

Mark followed the man back to the house, he could see another person inside the dimly lit house.

The man stopped at the door and told Mark to go in, the other person in the house looked at him and just nodded his head.

The man who let him in the door said,

'I'm Stan and that is Dave,..David' corrected the man in the form of an introduction without any indication of a handshake.

'I am Mark Crampton, I am working for Juliet Consolidated Enterprises, and to cut it short, my company want to buy your property'.

'Not for sale' was the simple reply from David who was still standing back in the shadows.

'You haven't heard the offer yet' said Mark wondering what planet these dudes were from.

'And you have the nerve to call me deaf, It's not for sale' said Stan.

'What sort of dollars was your company going to offer?' called out David.

Mark felt like responding with, fucking Australian dollars you fool. But he said calmly,

'What sort of dollars would you consider?'

'Tell your Company that fifty million would get us to the table for starters' said Stan.

Mark slowly shook his head and said that fifty million dollars would be way out of contention, to which Stan Strauss suggested he leave, but that he was welcome to camp by the river just down by the road, but no fires.

Mark thanked him and suggested that if they think of a realistic price by the morning and let him know. Stan Strauss just told him to 'fuck off'.

Mark arrived back in Cooktown quite late the next afternoon only to find that the caravan park was totally booked out due to the annual 'Cooktown Discovery Festival' held every June. Not knowing where to head he drove to Jason's house.

Jason was happy to see his friend Mark and when he heard about Mark having nowhere to park his caravan he insisted that he park it in the backyard and that he stay inside the house in the guest room.

They went over to the Sovereign Hotel for dinner but the place was packed and the restaurant was booked out they tried the RSL for dinner and the place was also packed out but as the manager knew Jason quite well he said he would organise a table for them.

Waiting for their meals to arrive and having a beer, Jason asked Mark if his trip had been successful, Mark told him the disappointing result he had as far as finding a property, and then laughingly told him about the two strange, to say the least, people that he had come across at a property called Watsonville and went on to tell him about the spikes that they, the Watsonville owners, had put into the track at one location and had been told that these spikes were also in other locations and that the owners did it to discourage trespasses on their property.

To Mark's amazement, Jason said that he had heard all about the strange vehicle traps and things like that around Watsonville and that he, when relieving at Laura Police Station, had actually visited Watsonville on more than one occasion following complaints about road spikes and bullet holes found in vehicles that have travelled along the gazetted roads across their property and that one of the owners, Stan Strauss had blamed the spikes being installed by organised gangs, as with the bullet holes, that were growing drugs around the area. Strauss had also told Jason that there were rumours of tents burnt at campsites. Stauss also said that both he and David Watson were fearful for their lives on occasions.

The next morning Jason had told Mark that he would be working extra hours that day due to the festival crowds and would not be home until about eight PM,

'The pub's and club's meal will be finished by then but I'll get a couple of rump steaks out of the freezer, what d'you reckon?'

'Fine by me, thanks Jason, I have a phone call to make and a report to write, and that's about me, a lazy day, but I will get some beer organised for this evening' replied Mark.

'You're a fucking legend mate! I'll see you later today' said Jason heading out the door.

Mark called Father Damien,

'Mark! How are you?' Asked the good Father.

'I'm good, Damo, but my news isn't great', Mark told Father Damien about his past weeks inspecting properties and the sad results, he told him about Watsonville and how ideal the property would be due to its size of around five hundred thousand acres and location with access from two directions, although it is only rated at fifteen acres per head of beef it could be improved quite easy to twelve or maybe ten. The Surveyor General has valued the leasehold at only just under one million dollars'.

'Well! That sounds very good Mark, have you offered a price to the owner?' Father Damien asked.

'They don't want to sell,' Mark replied.

'Everything is for sale my dear boy, it's just a matter of price, you need to find their price, it sounds like you have done all your homework on the property, at five hundred thousand acres, then maybe you should be offering up to the max, ten million isn't it? Do you think it would work at that price, Mark?'

'They were pretty adamant that it is not for sale' Mark emphasised, 'but' he continued, 'One of the owners said the negotiating start price would be fifty million'.

'Fifty million is five times the maximum amount that JCE is prepared to pay Mark, even if you got down to half of that price, as the property is around one hundred thousand acres more than what we are looking for, it may still be much too expensive, but at least you have a negotiating start price, that's something. Go back and talk to them and call me when you start negotiating.' Father Damien wasn't fazed at all.

'I can't call you from there unless I use their landline and that wouldn't be good, mobile phone reception ends out here almost as soon as I leave Cooktown' Mark advised.

'Can't you get a satellite telephone, don't they work up that way?' Father Damien asked.

Mark remembered that Terry had given him his Iridium phone number and to call him the next time he was around the area, so they must work out there.

'I hadn't thought of that', Mark replied, 'I'll get one organised and get back out there.'

Father Damien told Mark not to waste too much time, it was already over six months that he had been on the project and that JCE may get itchy if they don't get any reports and the next annual board meeting which is drawing close.

Mark advised Father Damien that he would get back out there ASAP and get back to him.

Mark called all three locations around Cooktown in the hope of obtaining a satellite telephone but to no avail, It seemed that the closest place he could get one was Cairns.

Mark started to put together his report on the property Watsonville Station.

It was around two o'clock that he remembered to get some beer for this evening, he walked up to the Sovereign and noticed the heat, even in June the temperature was twenty eight degree's centigrade, he decided he would have a schooner in the bar and then get a slab of stubbies from the bottle shop.

Owing to the festival there were quite a few people in the bar as Mark sat at the bar sipping his beer, a fellow sitting next to him who was dressed in denim jeans and a kaki Gundwana shirt asked Mark if he was 'up for the festival', Mark had replied no, that he was doing a bit of work here, but he didn't go into detail. And then, more of a courtesy Mark said to him.

'And you, are you up for the festival?' Knowing full well that he wouldn't be.

'Nar just finished mustering, I'll have a few weeks off and then probably do a bit of maintenance and a bit of work for Ergon, checking poles' the stranger said.

'Checking poles?' Mark queried.

'Yeah, with me chopper', helicopter that I use for mustering, I do contract mustering for a few places around here, generally start from April and finish up about now, before the wet and then there's typically a bit of work from the power company checking power poles in the hard to get at areas, it's a quid I suppose,' the stranger went on, 'Warren's me name, but everyone calls me Jacko' he concluded and reached out his hand.

Mark shook his hand and introduced himself whilst thinking what an interesting fellow this person seemed, then said.

'Another beer?' Mark asked, raising his empty glass.

The stranger picked up his almost empty schooner glass and said 'Why not, thanks' then drank the small amount of beer remaing as Mark ordered two more schooners from the lady behind the bar.

'Do you do any work for Watsonville?' Mark asked while waiting for the drinks to be served.

'Yeah, just finished mustering with the boys up there, d'yer know Stan, Dave?' Warren replied.

Mark told Warren that he did not know them but had met them just the day before yesterday when he was out there on a bit of business, he didn't say what business, but he said that he found them most unfriendly.

'They're alright, those boys,' was Warren's reply. They have been doing it tough up there and have been having their fair share of problems with people trespassing on their place and people growing plantations if you know what I mean'. Warren took a drink of his beer, 'Once you get to know 'em, you won't find nicer people. What sort of business do you want to do with them, are you a cattle buyer?'

'No…no, not a cattle buyer, I had a proposition to put towards them, that's all', Mark thought what the hell, this bloke might be able to help him.

Warren told Mark that they didn't like people to just 'drop in' and he said that he didn't blame them and told Mark that the only way to get around them, especially Stan, was to call them first, they are hard to get onto but just keep ringing until you get them.

Then, when you get them on the phone and you say you will be out there at such and such a time, ask them if they need anything bringing out and have a pen ready cos they will have a list of things. Then you will be right as they will be looking forward to seeing you as you will be bringing the stuff they need out and it saves them a big trip and time away from work.

'Oh, and they are very partial to a good bottle of scotch whiskey, My shout' said Warren ordering two more drinks.

As it turned out Warren had known both Stan and David for quite a long time, Warren's parents had a property close to theirs when it was owned and run by David's parents, then not long after Davids's parents had drowned in that tragic crossing, they had sold up and moved to Mareeba, much to Warrens disgust as he really missed living out there.

Mark finished his drink and said farewell to Warren and thanked him for the advice, Warren had told him that he was more than welcome and told him to just persist with those boys out at Watsonville and he'll be right.

Mark bought a slab of stubbies from the bottle shop and headed back to Jason's house, it was almost five o'clock and Mark was surprised to see Jason was home.

Jason said that it had been a fairly well behaved day and as extra coppers had been sent from Cairns his boss said that he could knock off for the day.

They sat at the outside table with a beer each and Mark told Jason that he was going to Cairns in the morning to buy a satellite telephone and that he would return in the afternoon then asked him if there was anything that he wanted bringing back from Cairns.

Jason asked Mark why he wanted a satellite phone and Mark told him that he needed to contact his boss while he was out in the field to get approval of things.

Jason had put down his beer and gone inside the house, he returned moments later with an Idium Extreme 9575 satphone.

'Here, you can borrow this for as long as you need to' Jason said as he passed the phone to Mark. 'You'll just have to set up your own account with Telstra, you can do that over the phone, your normal mobile that is'.

The next day Mark set up a Telstra account for the satellite telephone that Jason had loaned him. He then spent almost the rest of the day trying to call the landline phone number of Watsonville on his mobile phone but to no avail.

It wasn't until that night at nine o'clock, just after Jason had gone to bed for an early start the next morning, that when Mark tried calling the landline number again that it was answered.

'David speaking' said a mild voice

'Hello David, It's Mark Crampton, I was out there earlier this week with respect to making an offer on your property' Mark rushed to avoid letting David to get a word in, *such as* 'not interested', he continued 'I will be out there tomorrow at around three o'clock and wondered if you needed anything brought out from Cooktown?' There was an extended pause and then,

'Just a moment', David said and then laid the telephone handset down. Mark could hear footsteps and a door open and then distant voices, after quite some time just as he was about to hang up, he heard a distinct OK, and soon after David returned to the line,

'Do you have a pen?' He said.

'Yes' replied Mark anxiously. It was just like Warren had said.

The list of items that David had given to Mark was quite extensive and would require Mark to visit a number of Cooktown locations to fulfil the requirements.

It was almost eleven o'clock by the time Mark had finished running around Cooktown for the items on David Watson's list, there was only one item that was not available.

He was on his way to Watsonville and he calculated that it would be at least four o'clock by the time he got there, one hour later than he had told David, so be it! Mark thought, it was the best he could do. In his rushing around to get all the items, plus a bottle of Johnny Walker black label scotch whiskey, he had almost forgotten his purpose of the visit to Watsonville.

He had hooked up his caravan and had arrived at the Watsonville homestead at four thirty that afternoon and to his surprise, the dogs were on their chains. He opened the back of the canopy and started to take out the boxes containing David's items, there were four of them, the front door opened and Stan came out to the Landcruiser to help with the boxes. They both carried the four boxes into the house and placed them on top of the kitchen table, David appeared and asked Mark how much did he owe him and Mark replied he would get the receipts from the car.

He went back out to the cruiser and got the receipts and the bottle of Johnny Walker and returned to the house.

'Would anyone care for a drink?' Asked Mark lifting the bottle above his head.

'Suits me' David said, 'Just as soon as I fix up paying you, I'll need your bank details as I can only pay by phone banking, the internet is shit out here.

'You can count me in too' Stan said in a much better mood as he got three glasses from the bench.

Mark opened his bank account on his mobile to reveal his BSB number and his account number which he showed to David who wrote it down.

They all went outside in front of the house where a table and chairs stood under a big Flame Tree that was not in bloom at that time of the year. Stan poured two fingers of whiskey into each glass and passed a glass to Mark and then David, then holding his glass to chin height said 'Good Luck; as he sat in a chair, he looked at Mark,

'Thanks, Mark for bringing out that gear, much appreciated believe me and thanks for the drink too, you'll be staying for dinner I hope?'

Mark could not say yes fast enough and was thinking 'Thanks Warren' when Stan added,

'But firstly, get it straight, this place is not for sale for any amount of money to anyone...OK! So don't even ask and don't make any offers and we can all be really good friends'.

Mark was quite shocked, but on one hand, not really, Stan had put it straight forward to him, which in a way he respected, but he did feel a bit deflated and had no idea of what to say except OK.

'Look, Mark, if the property ever did go on the market, which of course it won't, then we would give you the first option to buy it' David added to Stan's comment. 'We want the lifestyle, not the money'.

What would we do with the money, live at the Gold Coast in a high rise apartment and drink ourselves to death?'

The barbequed tomahawk steaks were absolutely brilliant, David told Mark how he prepared them two hours before eating them by salting them generously with rock salt on each side to cause osmosis inside the steak which makes them very tender and does not make them taste salty.

Mark enjoyed the evening with Stan and David, they had a lot of yarn's to tell and also told him about the drug growers which they could do nothing about and it also seemed that the police couldn't either.

Stan told Mark he could camp by the river like he did last time, but reminded him 'No Fires!'

Mark asked Stan if he could fish in the river and Stan instantly said 'No!'

'We don't own the river, I know, but we own the land that you 'Have' to walk on to get to the river, that's the way it is, we just don't want anyone on the property and we don't think that is a lot to ask, and sorry, but we don't make exceptions and that includes you'. The change in Stan was incredible, he was becoming quite chatty and seemed even friendly over dinner, but now he had reverted back to the person that he was when he had first arrived at Watsonville Station.

David added 'If we catch anyone fishing we will have a writ of trespass issued, we have the right to ask them for identification for that purpose'. David was also becoming unfriendly and for no apparent reason.

'If we see a car parked anywhere on our property we have a writ of trespass issued to the car registration address' Stan concluded. 'If we let you go fishing today it will be shooting tomorrow and then bringing your mates up here and before we know it there are people up here everywhere and bush fires all over the place, no way!'

Mark decided that it was time to say goodnight to this pair.

Mark camped by the river that night, he went to bed thinking that this pair of station owners were certainly different, strange people indeed he thought.

The next morning Mark called Father Damien and told him briefly about the conversation last night and told him that it seemed that they would not be able to buy Watsonville for whatever price JCE put on it.

Father Damien also thought that these people must be a bit strange to knock back such an offer on a somewhat, from what Mark had described to him, run down property and homestead.

He told Mark to get it all in writing to him and to start looking at properties further west of Cooktown.

Mark headed back to Cooktown feeling somewhat disappointed but on the other hand he was looking forward to exploring new territory to the west.

Father Damien had called the other member of the board who was assisting him in seeking properties suitable for JCE's new venture.

Carl Stephenson was not overly surprised when he heard the results of the negotiations with cattle stations in the Far North and most particularly in the response from Watsonville Station.

'I'm sure that you will have a trick or two to pull out of your bag Carl' father Damien had said as he hung up the telephone.

Carl Stephenson called Kirill Nikolaev, he let the phone ring for about three rings and then hung up waiting for a call from 'Nik'.

● ● ● ● ● ● ● ●

The Fishing Trip

Mark had returned to Cooktown later that day and had again parked his caravan in Jason's backyard, Jason had returned home from work at around five PM and they both went over to the Sovereign for a few beers and then a meal.

Mark had told Jason the result of the proposition that he had put to Strauss and Watson and mentioned that he thought they were different sorts of blokes and he told of the mood change when he asked if he could go fishing on their property and the savage reaction by both of them.

Jason was aware that they went out of their way to keep trespassers out of the property, even to the extent of using their mustering choppers to find them and chase them away.

Jason told Mark that he had to go to Cairns the next morning to attend the preliminary hearing on the car theft gang and the truckie Steve Brown and that he may be gone for about four days, but he reminded Mark that he was more than welcome to stay in the house while he was gone.

Mark thanked him and said it would be easier to use his kitchen table to write his reports to JCE. He also said that Jason's Iridium sat phone was in his car, locked in a concealed, safe place, and he would grab it for him on their way back to Jason's place as he had no need for it anymore.

Both drinking a stubby and talking on the way back to Jason's, they forgot to get the sat phone out of his car for Jason that night.

It was the second day that Jason had been in Cairns that Mark got a call from Terry asking if he would be interested in a fishing trip, Terry had said that they would go tomorrow, Saturday and be going for about two days and would be camping on the river bank so he would need his swag.

Mark thought that would be a great idea, he had just finished and sent off his report to JCE and a fishing break would be just perfect, It was Saturday tomorrow and Jason was due back on Sunday. Mark told Terry he would be there tomorrow just after lunch.

Terry Andrews and David Barnes had parked their Nissan Patrol just far away from the Watsonville Station homestead so they could see that the old Nissan Ute that Stauss and Watson used to get around the property was not parked where it usually was near the machinery shed. Terry had assumed that they would be pretty busy drafting cattle up at their yards which were about fifteen kilometres away from the homestead.

David waited in the Nissan while Terry walked down the track to the homestead, David had a view of the track behind the homestead for roughly two kilometres, should the Strauus-Watson patrol come down this track heading towards the homestead he was to sound the horn, just one quick blast.

There was only one dog that had been left at the homestead and it was fast asleep and as Terry could see was on a chain.

He went to the front door and reached up above the door and onto the top of the door frame where they left the key each time they locked the door. Terry had seen them do this purely by accident when he was scouting around their place one afternoon and they had returned from around the property somewhere and had unlocked the door, one of them had gone into the house to collect something and then when leaving the house had relocked the door and replaced the key.

Terry was now inside the house and looked quickly for the firearms that he knew had to be in there somewhere.

He found the bedrooms and in one bedroom a Tikka .270 rifle leaned against the wall in one corner opposite the unmade bed, he checked the next bedroom which had only a mattress on the floor without bedding, lying on this bed were all sorts of things, fishing rods, landing nets, a sleeping bag and a singe barrel twelve gauge shotgun. In the next bedroom on a wall mounted gun rack were a Savage pump action shotgun and a Marlin lever action 30-30 rifle, The shotgun was loaded with four AAA shot cartridges and the rifle seemed to be loaded but he could not see how many rounds were inside the tubular magazine.

Terry worked the rifle's lever over the unmade bed and ejected five 30-30 rounds, he quickly reloaded them back into the rifle and then left the house carrying the shotgun and the rifle, leaning them against the wall outside the front door he carefully locked the door and returned the key to the top of the door frame in the exact place that he had found it, picking up the weapons he returned to David waiting in the Nissan.

'That was fucking tense mate, sitting here watching, it seemed that you were gone for fucking hours', Barnsy said.

'It was no fucking picnic in that fucking brothel of a place either pal', replied Terry, 'It fucking stank inside that house and that fucking dog would not stop barking, I was expecting to hear you on the horn at any time, plus the fucking stink inside that place, I don't know how they live in there.

The next day, Saturday, Mark met David and Terry at their lease and it was decided to take only Terry's Nissan Patrol wagon as it was big enough for all of them plus the tree swags on the roof rack with the fishing rods, leaving plenty of room in the back for the three esky's and gas cooker plus various bits and pieces.

They were all enjoying a stubby as they drove along the road back in the direction towards Laura for about nine kilometres where they found a hardly visible track to the left.

The track was extremely rough and overgrown and Terry became lost several times and told Mark that he had not been down here in a while.

Mark was of the opinion that no one had been down this way for quite some time but he kept it to himself as these guys seemed to know what they were doing and had said that it was well worth the effort to get to this place as the fishing was great and it was out of the way with little chance of being seen.

They were now going down a very steep and very rough section and Mark was glad that they weren't in his Landcruiser.

They had arrived at the bottom of the track and the river was just in view. Terry had said that they could go no further and that they should all walk down to the river and look for a campsite.

They were ready to go when Terry slid the rifle from behind the back seat and Mark gave him an enquiring look,

'Crocks mate, the pricks lay around the banks and I don't want to be their dinner' responded Terry.

They walked down to the river bank and turned to walk upstream of the river toward a towering rocky outcrop on both sides. It wasn't long before it turned into a gorge and they had to leave the river to climb up the slope to go around a point in the river.

Mark had somehow become in the lead in front of Terry and David was last in line, Terry lowered the loaded 30-30 rifle level with the back of Mark's neck and pulled the trigger.

The explosion of the rifle shot reverberated around the gorge, at around one hundred and seventy decibels it was quite deafening, but Mark would not have heard it, he was dead before he hit the boulders they were climbing over.

Terry, wearing disposable gloves, had taken a hand towel from his pocket together with a freezer bag, he dabbed the towel in the puddle of blood that had formed next to Mark's throat and then placed it into the freezer bag. They then went through his pockets and took the keys to his Landcruiser. Then they removed his R M Williams boots,

There was a large hole that had been formed by three large jagged rocks just near where Mark's body lay and it was little effort to push his body head first into the hole where the body fell for about three metres or more. It was deep enough decided Barnsy and Terry dropped the rifle down into the hole.

They returned to the Nissan and, still wearing disposable gloves, took one of Mark's fishing rods and from his backpack took his mobile telephone, one of his iPod earphones, a fishing knife in a sheath, his hat and a pair of leg gators together with the shotgun.

These items were also dropped into the hole containing Mark's body.

Other items, the remaining iPod earphone and a small pocket knife they took with them

Terry Andrews and David Barnes had then driven to the fishing spot where they had enjoyed fishing and lunching with Mark Crampton a few weeks prior and, again wearing disposable gloves, they set up camp being careful to place Mark's swag in position near the fireplace unroll it and make look like it had been slept in. His esky was also placed in the camp as with his backpack with some clothing removed and placed on top of the backpack his spare fishing rod was laid on his 'slept in' swag along with some clothing from his bag.

David Barnes had gone fishing while Terry made a campfire and, wearing gloves, set up utensils and plates for three people, it was just starting to go dark by the time they had eaten a feed of fish and canned baked beans ensuring all three plates had been used but not cleaned, as with the utensils.

Six of Mark's beers were drunk and the empties were placed in a pile with Terry and Barnsy's empties.

They spent a quiet night camped beside the river and the next morning, leaving the campsite undisturbed they drove to their lease and unlocked Mark's Landcruiser to look for any valuables and money. Wearing disposable gloves they found Mark's wallet locked in the glove box, there was approximately two hundred dollars in his wallet which they left intact as with his credit cards. They also found in the glove box three thousand dollars in one hundred dollar notes and a sat phone, these items they took and then relocked the Landcruiser and took the keys with them for disposal.

They had driven back to the river just after lunch and had parked close to their camp, Barnsy, wearing Mark's boots and carrying his own boots with him, then walked up and along the river making sure to make footprints in the sand with both pairs of boots and then with Mark's boots only up and over the track beside the river and down a gully where a creek meets the river he stopped at a grassy area and removed Mark's boots.

Wearing his disposable gloves he took the blood soaked towel from the freezer bag and carefully wiped it on and around the grassed area, he then carefully placed the pocket knife onto the grassed area that was covered in blood ensuring that some blood went onto and into the crevices in the pocket knife, he then did the same with the one iPod earphone but well away from the pocket knife.

He then set fire to the grassed area which burned very rapidly being dry, taking off his shirt, he wafted the flames over the blooded area so they extinguished before completely burning the area.

Carrying Mark's boots and wearing socks only on his feet Barnsy very carefully moved off the grassed area and onto the creek gravel and down to the river back toward the camp where he could then safely remove his socks and walk barefoot back to the camp.

It was about five o'clock in the afternoon that Terry had driven to a neighbouring property that was about an hour's drive and had used the property's landline telephone to report the shooting to the police.

Jason had not become aware of the shooting until he had reported for duty at nine o'clock on the following Monday morning when he read the brief about the shooting call last night, he didn't relate the shooting with Mark and wasn't until later that day when Mark had not returned to Cooktown that Jason had informed his sergeant that his friend had gone fishing and that he had not returned as yet although a note that he had left in Jasons' house had indicated that he would be back at around five PM Sunday, yesterday. His name, he told the sergeant was Mark Crampton.

When the sergeant informed the officer in charge of the investigation, Detective Sergeant Cameron Jamison, at the Mareeba Police Station the officer had confirmed that the missing man's name was Mark but that his surname was unknown to his friends. The missing man's vehicle had been left at his companion's mining lease and a crew from the scene were going there this morning to get an identification on the vehicle's owner via the number plate.

The sergeant told Jason that the missing man's name was Mark but that a surname was not available at this stage.

'Looks very much like it's your mate', the sergeant told Jason, they want two more of our boys out there this afternoon to help with the search and I was going to send you, but that can't happen now for obvious reasons'.

Jason was now feeling quite shattered and even more so towards the late afternoon when it was confirmed that the vehicle left at the mining lease was registered to Mark Crampton.

Jason had at about five thirty that afternoon received a call from Detective Sergeant Jamison asking what was his relationship with Mark Crampton,

'I met him about two months ago when he came in to report an assault and the theft of his vehicle here in Cooktown' replied Jason and continued with a brief report about the exposure of the stolen vehicle group operating in FNQ. He didn't hear back from the detective again.

After a few weeks and the talk about the shooting and the missing person had died to almost no mention.

A tilt tow truck had taken Mark's caravan from Jason's backyard and Mark's vehicle had been collected from the mining lease, these had been relocated at the police storage yard in Mareeba and would be held in evidence.

As the search for a body continued at Watsonville the whole of the property was declared a crime scene and any movement with the property was under the supervision of the police.

The mustered cattle in the yards had been released back into the property by a caretaker who had been appointed to look after the stock on the property for the time being.

• • • • • • • •

In the following few months It was basically back to normal for Jason except for being promoted to sergeant and being transferred to Officer in Charge at Laura Police Station which quite suited him and served there for just over twelve months when he had a win on the 'Oz Lotto' of a little over four million dollars.

Jason had resigned from the Queensland Police and bought a unit on the Gold Coast in Queensland following his win.

• • • • • • • •

The Alleged Shooting Aftermath

The court case for Strauss and Watson was held as a combined case and had been to the Supreme Court of Queensland at Cairns listed as R v Strauss & Watson.

Jason Walsh was subpoenaed to attend the trial at the Cairns Court as a witness for the prosecution, it had been over a year since the disappearance of Mark Crampton and both the accused had been remanded since the day of the alleged shooting at The Lotus Glen Correctional Centre located just eighty six kilometres from Cairns.

Jason was asked how he had met Mark Crampton and how well did he know him, he was asked if Mark had told him why he was in Cooktown and Jason had said that he was a property scout for a company called JCE and was looking at properties in the area with a view to purchase.

'Did Mark Crampton ever visit Watsonville Station in respect to his business?' asked the prosecuting barrister.

'Yes he did' Jason answered

'On how many occasions?'

'Err..two,.. I think, or maybe it was three' Jason was trying to remember.

'Was it two, or was it three?' Queried the prosecutor.

'It's quite a while ago now and I am not sure, it was no big deal, I knew he was just busy with his work', answered Jason.

'Did he make any comments about the owners of Watsonville Mr Walsh?'

'It was following his last visit that he thought they were a bit strange and from being quite friendly towards him they had turned quite aggressive when he had asked if he could fish on their property. They had told him that he could neither fish nor shoot on their property and to keep off their property or he would receive a writ of trespass from them'. Jason replied.

'Have you met the owners of Watsonville Mr Walsh?' The prosecutor then asked.

'Yes, on a number of occasions' replied Jason.

'And what were the circumstances of those occasions?'

'It was when as a member of the Queensland Police that I had cause to talk to them in respect to complaints from people who had been chased by them, the property owners, from their property where the complainants had suffered personal or property damage' Jason recalled.

'Did Mark Crampton ever mention to you the names of Terry Andrews and David Barnes?'

'He did mention them, but only their given names, I don't think he told me about their surnames and I think he referred to David as 'Barnsy' once or twice'. Said Jason trying to remember.

'Did Mark Crampton tell you how he had met with these two, Terry Andrews and David Barnes?'

'Yes, Mark Crampton's vehicle had got stuck on a spike, as I recall, and they came along and helped him I think and he must have kept in touch with them as far as I know. Again trying to remember Jason had said.

'Did he tell you that he was going fishing with Andrews and Barnes?' The prosecutor then asked.

'No, I was in Cairns when he decided to go fishing with them, he was staying with me at that time and he had left a note saying that he was away fishing and would return on Sunday afternoon'. Jason explained.

'That will be all thank you, Mr Walsh'. Said the prosecutor.

The defence did not wish to cross examine Jason and he was free to leave, he decided to sit in the public gallery and listen to more of the evidence against the accused.

The next witness to take the stand was Warren Jackson.

'Mr Jackson, did you ever meet Mark Crampton?' The prosecutor started.

'I did yes, one time only you mind, at the Sovereign Hotel in Cooktown, sir' he answered.

'And are you familiar with both of the accused?'

'I am, yes sir'.answered Warren Jackson

'What capacity do you know the accused Mr Jackson?'

'I fly with them and help at mustering time, we, Stan and David and meself, all fly choppers and do the mustering for most of the properties around that area of Watsonville, for a price like!' Offered Warren Jackson.

'Did Mr Crampton enquire to you about the accused, the owners of Watsonville Station?' The prosecutor wanted to know.

'He did, he said that he had tried to approach them at their property, unannounced mind you, and thought that they were arseholes, pardon your honour,' said Warren glancing at the judge.

'Did you advise Mr Crampton how to approach the accused at their property?'

'He wouldn't tell me exactly what it was that he wanted to talk to them about but said it was very important to him so I told him how they appreciated people calling them on the telephone before going out to the property and that they would welcome the offer to collect supplies for them from town to bring outwith them. I also told him that they were very partial to good scotch whiskey' Warren Jackson told the court.

The next witness was Father Damien Downes.

'What is your relationship with the missing man Mark Crampton?' Asked the prosecutor.

'I was Mark's school teacher in Canberra and had been more like a second father to him in his growing up and had lately engaged him with employment in the company that I am a board director', the very well spoken Father Damien replied.

'In what capacity was Mr Crampton employed and why was he based in Cooktown?, Father'. Asked the prosecutor.

'Mark was employed as a consultant analyst and was engaged in a feasibility study of the area west of Cooktown.

'Did Mr Crampton's job involve meeting with the owners of Watsonville?'

'Yes, and other property owners in the district, my company was desirous to do business with property owners in the region'. Said Father Damien.

'Did Mr Crampton mention to you about his meeting with the accused?'

'Mark had said that one minute the Watsonville Station owners were quite receptive and then the other minute they became quite aggressive and I advised Mark to discontinue any negotiations with them'. Father Damien answered.

'That will be all thank you, Father'. Was the prosecutor's response.

It was obvious to Jason that the prosecution was portraying both Watson and Strauss as agressive and using these witnesses, including himself, to confirm this.

He knew the rest of the court case would be too boring and too long for him and it would bring back sad memories so he left the courthouse and before flying back to the Gold Coast he decided to hire a car and visit his old friends in Cooktown.

Things had not changed in the eighteen months since Jason had been in Cooktown with the exception that a new Officer in Charge had been installed at the police station. The Senior Sergeant when Jason was stationed there was a great fellow named Ken Marsden who had retired from the police and was now working as a ranger and was based at Coen.

It had been an accidental 'meet up' with Ken at the RSL club. Ken had come into Cooktown to get a few things, one of them being a satellite telephone which he could not get anywhere around Cooktown, he was staying the night and thought a few beers and a meal at the club before an early night was the plan.

Jason had said to Ken that he had a sat phone which he hadn't used for yonks and that he was welcome to have it and that he would send it to him once he returned to his unit, that's if he was in no rush.

Ken had thanked Jason for the kind offer, but he had that afternoon ordered one from Brisbane and he would have it sometime next week.

Ken had told Jason that he was really enjoying his job as a ranger as there was very little pressure attached to the job, unlike the police force, he was, however, amazed at the amount of drugs that he had found growing around the district.

The police had seized the entire property known as Watsonville Station and the Public Trustee had organised a cattle muster and sale, the trustee then had the property evaluated and valued by the Valuer General.

Due to the complexity of the situation, it was a further two years before the trustee placed the property on the market for public auction at a venue in Mareeba.

JCE had instructed a local real estate agent Vincent Villani to attend the auction and bid for the property on their behalf.

Villani placed the successful bid of six point three million dollars on the property on behalf of JCE.

JCE created a new company, Watsonville Pastoral & Mining Proprietary Limited, also known as WPM. This company leased the property of Watsonville Station from JCE for a staggering amount of ten million dollars per annum and took out a trading loan of twenty million dollars which was guaranteed by JCE. This loan was to introduce fifteen thousand head of breeding stock onto Watsonville Station and for pasture improvement including self mustering yards in various locations, the establishment of accommodation buildings and access roads.

Part of the Watsonville business plan was to produce and sell fifteen thousand head of beef cattle for a gross profit of thirty five, million dollars within twenty four months, this was achieved, and this figure would grow as more breeding areas could be brought online.

At the time of purchasing Watsonville, it was estimated to be able to carry breeders at fifteen acres per head, it was estimated to have increased the carrying capacity of Watsonville to twelve acres per head within two years of careful management and had now forecast an increase of beef cattle sales to twenty thousand head at approximately forty eight million dollars gross sales.

The board members of JCE were quite happy with the trading results of WPM, the lease alone was contributing one point six million dollars to each of the shareholders and the net profits were also now returning another four million to each shareholder.

The shareholders in this instance were the six members of the board of JCE and other companies under JCE were also contributing excellent returns for its members.

The loss of Mark Crampton had put a heavy shadow over the project and all were quite saddened about the event, but as Father Damien had expressed to them 'Life must go on'.

• • • • • • • •

The Satellite Telephone

Jason Walsh had decided to move from the bustling Gold Coast to somewhere a little quieter and with a bit more room and no neighbours.

He had been living off the interest of the investments he had made with the lotto winnings and decided to change some of those investments into a small cattle property that he could manage on his own and his new partner Narelle, whom he had met about a year previous and had now been living with him in his unit for the past ten months, she too wanted to get out of the rat race and go bush.

They had found a small property of three hundred acres near a small town called Monto, which is about five hundred and fifty kilometres from Brisbane and were busy packing for the move.

Jason was taking things from his top drawer and packing them into a carton when he came across the note that Mark had left for him while he was away in Cairns.

He had kept the note, which said that 'he had gone fishing and would be back on Sunday' in case it was required for evidence, which it wasn't, but for some reason he had kept it.

Seeing the note had brought to Jason's mind the sat phone which he had offered to give to Ken Marsden in Cooktown, he now wondered where it was and made a mental note whilst packing to look for it.

Everything was packed and had been picked up by the removalist with smaller items placed in his car, but he did not recall seeing the sat phone and it now played on his mind.

They had moved into the home near Monto and everything was going well, they were about to commence stocking the property and working out a plan to visit cattle sales around the area when Jason suddenly remembered loaning the sat phone to Mark and it became more important to him to try to go back in his memory to what happened to the sat phone than to buy cattle, much to the annoyance of Narelle.

He had remembered loaning it to Mark just before his second meeting with Watson and Strauss as he needed to contact his boss whilst at Watsonville, yes he could visualise that quite clearly.

When Mark returned from the meeting he gave the sat phone back to Jason…yes..? 'No!…they were in the pub,…' Jason said aloud, 'We were going to get it from his Landcruiser on the way back to my house from the pub!'

The satellite telephone was in the Landcruiser, where did the Landcruiser go after it was picked up by the police?

Jaso called the Mareeba Police Station and asked for Detective Sergeant Cameron Jamison.

'You mean Inspector Jamison' the lady had said.

'Yes, that would be him' Jason said.

'Who is calling please', he was asked.

'It's Ja...It's former Senior Constable Jason Walsh from The Cooktown Police,' Jason thought that it may be easier for Cameron to remember him by his old title.

After a short wait, 'Jason! How are you, mate? I heard you won the lottery and pissed off' bellowed the voice of Cameron Jamison.

'Yeah, and now you are an inspector, congratulations Cameron'.

They chatted about old times and then Cameron asked Jason the reason he had called him.

'Stupid question, but when you guys searched the ute of the missing bloke at Watsonville a while back, did you come across a sat phone?' Jason asked.

How the fuck would I know?' Laughed Cameron. 'Why? Would you want to know that?'

'I loaned Mark, the guy who went missing, my sat phone and I am pretty sure it was in the Landcruiser, just wondered that's all' said Mark.

'Yeah, they are pretty exy items, Jason, I can understand that you would want it back, there will be a complete list of items that were in the vehicle and I'll see if I can find it and send it to you. What's your email?'

Jason gave Cameron his email and after a little more reminiscing hung up.

The email arrived two days later, it was a complete inventory of items that were found in Mark Crampton's Landcruiser after it was brought in from the mining lease of Andrews and Barnes. The satellite telephone was not listed.

In the bottom right hand side of the inventory was the name, date and signature of the person that searched the vehicle and as fate would have it, it was a colleague of Jason's from the training days in Townsville. He called the Mareeba Police Station again and this time asked for Senior Constable Grant Simmons,

'Sergeant Simmons is not available just now, can I take a message, or get him to call you back' the lady asked, Jason left his name and mobile number and it was only a matter of minutes before he received a return call.

'Hey Jase, long time no see' said Grant eagerly.

They exchanged some banter about the Townsville Police Academy and where they had been and so on.

'Mate!' Said Jason, 'The Crampton Landcruiser you did the search on about four years ago.'

'That's going back, but I do remember that one, the salvage team had a lot of trouble getting it on the truck as the vehicle was locked and they had to spray silicone on the tyres to get it off when they got here.' Replied Grant.

'So, nobody got into the car before you?' Asked Jason.

'Don't think so, it was thought that the keys were with the missing owner, we ended up finding the spare set of keys in his caravan. Why do you ask?' Continued Grant.

'It's a bit of a story, but I actually knew the guy and he was staying with me when he went missing, the short of it is, he had my sat phone in his car when he disappeared and it now looks like it has also disappeared'. Jason told Grant and he had suggested searching for the sat phone through the phone's manufacturer, he had done it previously and if Jason could give him the information of the manufacturer, where purchased, what date and serial number, then they could search for it and tell you the last time it was used and it's location, and strangely they don't need the phone number to do it.

Grant gave Jason his email and said to send him the sat phone's details and he would see what could be done, he also gave Jason his mobile number so he would not have to go through the station switch which recorded all conversations.

Narelle had been patient while Jason had been doing his bit of investigation but now thought she should remind him that they were supposed to be buying some cattle and plans were made for the following Monday.

The next day Jason received a text message from Grant telling him that the sat phone had been used just three days ago from latitude 'sixteen degrees, five minutes and twelve seconds South, one hundred and forty two degrees' forty four minutes East. Where the Vehicle was collected from?

Jason immediately checked the coordinates that placed the location near the Mitchell River, he hadn't been to the mining lease on Watsonville but he knew it was around that location. He knew that Mark would not have sold the sat phone nor would he have loaned it as it was not his, had he left it at the lease accidentally and the lease owners Andrews and Barnes were using the phone. Jason thought about contacting the police but then decided that it was not really a police matter and he doubted that they would be interested, he would check this out personally.

Narelle was horrified when Jason said he was going up the Mitchell River to check on his sat phone,

'Surely...surely, it would be cheaper just to buy a new one' she said to Jason and her anger was starting to show.

Jason poured a couple of drinks and took her out to the front verandah where they sat in the sun and he told her the story of Mark Crampton.

She said that she completely understood and said that she would go with him, Jason had at first objected but when she said that she was not going to hang around here on her own, he changed his mind.

They only had a BMW X5 and a Hilux SR5, and decided to pack the SR5 for the journey from Monto to Laura, one thousand and seven hundred kilometres.

They were booked into the Lakeland Downs Hotel at Laura, they had come via Cairns and Cooktown where they had spent a night at each and Narelle just loved Cairns to the extent that Jason had promised that they would spend some time there on the way back.

Using his newly bought Hema X2 navigation system he had left Narelle at the hotel and had set off towards the mining lease on the off chance that Andrews and Barnes would be out there.

He had remembered Mark's warning about the spikes just after the turnoff and slowed to a snail's pace but it seemed that the spikes had been removed.

He didn't quite get to the lease when he met an old Nissan Patrol coming towards him and he pulled over to the left as much as he could and stopped.

The Nissan Patrol containing two people, who Jason guessed were Andrews and Barnes, pulled up level with him and the driver asked him if he was lost,

'I might be', Jason answered, 'I am looking for Terry Andrews'

'Never heard of him mate! what would you want him for anyway.' Said the driver.

'I think he has my satellite telephone and I want it back' Jason said, he had thought hard about how to approach these people and thought that going straight to the point might be the best.

'We aint got no satellite telephone up here' the driver' stated.

'Strange, the satellite company gave me this location, they said it was being used here!' Jason said quite calmly.

'He sold it to me!' The person in the passenger seat called out loudly and unexpectedly.

'Shut up dickhead' quipped the driver.

'Who sold it to you?' Jason asked quickly.

'A bloke that used to work for us, he owed us money and sold his phone to us, can't remember his name but I always thought that the phone was hot. Nicked it from you eh?' The driver took over the conversation from the passenger. 'We haven't got it anymore, Charlie here dropped it in the river last week!'

Jason guessed that he could be in a dangerous situation and cut the talk short, 'Ah well, no good going any further up then, seems that it is lost, so be it, thanks anyway fellers, I'll just find a place to turn around'.

The two occupants waited and watched until the stranger turned around and they watched as he returned down the track that he had come from.

'Where the fuck did you get that fucking phone from?' Barnsy asked Terry,

'I found it in his truck when I went through it' replied Terry.

'And you fucking kept it, you fucking drongo, I had just assumed it was your phone' Barnsy said shaking his head. "We'd better be careful now if this thing is linked to us.

Terry responded, 'The bloke didn't seem too upset when we told him it was now in the river'.

'And that's where it had better go' Barnsy said quite pissed off at Terry, he thought he was a lot smarter than that.

Barnsy told Terry that he thought that the bloke was a copper just scouting and that he probably recorded the conversation about the phone and that he would take it back to analyse it. Terry told him he was getting paranoid and not to worry.

Jason had recorded the whole conversation from when the Nissan driver had asked if he was lost. It was sad that he could do nothing more until he returned Narelle to their home in Monto, but it had been nearly four years now and a couple more weeks wouldn't hurt.

Once back home the first person that Jason called with the news of the sat phone was Inspector Cameron Jamison and he explained to Cameron that the phone may be linked somehow to the disappearance of Mark Crampton for the following reasons.

(1) Mark had told Jason that the sat phone was safely locked up in a concealed place in his Landcruiser

(2) Mark would not have sold the sat phone as it was not his and Mark was not short of money, he always

seemed to have money as he was being paid exceptional money from his employment.

(3) How did Terry Andrews come into possession of the phone if Mark's car was locked and no keys could be found in his backpack and it was presumed that Mark had the keys on him when he disappeared?

Inspector Jamison had listened to Jason without once interrupting him, but once Jason had finished talking, Jamison told him that he was wasting both of their time as the the two people who were responsible for Crampton's murder, had been found guilty and were now both serving life sentences in prison, the case was closed some time ago and it is now history.

Jason had detected a tone in Cameron Jamison that was not there before when he had called him the other day, something was not right.

Jason then called Grant Simmons on his mobile, there was no answer and the call went straight to Grant's message bank.

Grant called back just minutes later.

'Jason..what the fuck is going on, Jamison revved the fuck out of me a couple of days ago about this fucking sat phone, apparently for some reason he had gone looking for our conversation through the station switchboard and told me not to communicate with you in respect to the closed case of the missing Crampton man and not to bring up this conversation with anyone. I don't think he is aware of the report that I received from the satellite telephone company just yesterday' said Grant.

'Yeah, I just spoke to him a little while ago and he sounded quite alienated, say,..what report from the sat phone company? Do you mean the location?'

'I also asked for a call record for the last five years and they sent me through a report on the numbers dialled and the numbers received, I suppose you would like a copy, I'll email it to you tonight from my home computer, got to go', and Grant ended the call.

The email showed all the calls made and received by that satellite telephone for the period before Jason had loaned the phone to Mark which showed some calls that Jason had made, it showed the only call that Mark had made according to the dates and then just after Mark's disappearance, it showed a number of calls made to a number that had never answered followed by a received call within an hour after making the call from the same regional communications tower as the unanswered calls.

The report also showed a call to the same number that was never answered at about the same time that Jason had fronted the guys in the Nissan and had then reported a call from the same communication tower just minutes later.

Jason thought he could understand what might be happening when he studied the report, but he wanted a second opinion.

Narelle's brother James, was visiting them next week and he was a communications technical engineer, Jason wanted James to have a look at the sat phone company report and see what he could make of it.

In the interim Narelle was pushing Jason every day to get the cattle thing happening as she was bored shitless.

Jason had no intention of leaving his newfound investigation and he suggested that she visit the Gym or something in Monto just while he got this thing of his sorted, she unhappily informed him that there was 'Fuck all' in Monto and that she may as well head back to the Gold Coast,

'You said you had had enough of the Gold Coast so we agreed to come here' Jason said.

'Yeah,..and you said we would get into growing beef cattle, not turning into a private fucking investigator' Narelle had angrily responded.

It suddenly came to Jason, 'Why not set up a gym in town, you said there was nothing there, could be filling a big gap, what do you think?'

'Wow!...that could be good, but… you are too busy' she said.

'I really meant You!.. You could do it and I'll bet you would enjoy it' Jason said as he thought that she sounded half keen.

'But once it is set up I don't want to hang around it all day' said Narelle sounding a little less positive.

'You would employ someone to run it, simple. Jason solved that one! And Narelle started research instantly on the internet.

James had arrived on Friday afternoon and by seven o'clock that evening, he was pouring through the sat phone report and was becoming as interested as Jason was.

It seems that since Mark had possession of the phone, he made one call, and he highlighted it on the copy that Jason had made, but then it seems that at least once a month this phone has called this unanswered number and that this phone has received a call from different numbers within one hour from calling the number that never answers and from the same tower that the unanswered call went to.

The number of the return calls is varied but only five times, so in this period each of the five numbers has called the sat phone nine times and the unanswered number has been called five times that amount, forty five times.

The unanswered call duration time hardly varies, which means it rings for the same amount of times with each call, like a code, Jason had asked James,

'Exactly, the number that the sat phone is calling alerts someone to make contact with the sat phone caller and they do, obviously with a different number but one that is not identified by caller ID' James explained.

'Can we find out where it is?' Jason asked.

'I can find out where the tower is and then we can look at the tower's range and the signal strength of the outgoing call to the unanswered number and calculate it by percentage on a map within the radius of the tower to determine its actual distance from the tower, but that's probably as far as we can go without a warrant from the police, can you get one Jason?' James outlined the system.

'No, I don't think that I can, the police are not the least interested' Jason told James.

James finished his drink and said that there are ways, but they are illegal.

James went into detail with Jason on how a scanner can follow the direction of a mobile phone from a transmitting tower but not so from a receiving tower.

Firstly you need the type of scanner and you need to know the transmitting mobile number and the receiving tower location, which we do, he added but then the hard thing is, it can only be traced while it is transmitting.

'You have a scanner! Jason asked excitedly.

'I do', answered James, 'But we would have to be in the tower's range area to use it'.

James had worked out the location of the tower which was in Gladstone and the signal strength of the outgoing call registered seventy eight percent, which would make scanning a lot easier than if it was lesser.

All they had to do was be in Gladstone at any location within twenty kilometres from the tower with all the Five numbers that had been recorded by the sat phone, locked into the scanner, if any of those numbers dialled out on a call the scanner would locate the equipment to within ten metres.

So all it will really do is tell you at what address the equipment is that is dialling out to the sat phone, for whatever that would be worth'. Commented James, 'Will that really prove anything for you?'

'Probably not', conceded Jason, 'But it won't hurt to have a look at the place that's communicating with the boys at the mining lease, which I would think is more of a plantation than a mining lease.

James looked rather confused so Jason got more drinks and then told James the whole story as far as he knew it and ended by saying that he thought that Strauss and Watson had been set up, he had no idea why, but he also thought that Andrews and Barnes may be the answer but he had very little to go on. He also thought that it was very strange that the police did not want to know about it, or that's how it seemed.

Looking back at the sat phone records it seemed around the third of every month and always between ten o'clock and twelve noon in the morning, very consistent they agreed. And decided to meet at a football field in Gladstone on the third of next month, which was a Tuesday, and see if they could get the scanner into operation.

The morning of the third day of the following month found Jason meeting up with James at the little park near the council depot which was close to the tower, it was almost ten o'clock and James had superimposed the Gladstone map onto his scanner and had calibrated the location to within five metres.

He had not long finished the map calibration when one of the five numbers registered and almost immediately the scanner placed a red marker onto the map. This was the location of the unit transmitting a call to the tower for a satellite transfer.

The address showing on the scanner was in the CBD on Chaple Street, they drove to the address to discover that it was an office building that housed one company, Northern Trading and Logistics.

As they drove past the office building, two bikies were parking their Harley Davidsons in the car park area that had a sign 'Staff Parking Only', they drove on innocently and found a Maccas for some breakfast.

Jason had only a one hundred and sixty kilometre drive to his home in Monto, after an hour and a half he was already doing a company search of Northern Trading and Logistics to discover that it was a subsidiary of The Northern Hotels Pty Ltd and the company director is Carl Stephenson.

A subsequent search showed that The Northern Hotels company is part of the JCE group of companies.

'Now that *is* interesting; said Jason to James who had followed Jason back to Monto to spend the balance of the week helping his sister put the gym together in town.

It just seemed to Jason to be a strange coincidence that this company, that Mark's employer was associated with, was in contact with the mining lease on Watsonville Station.

That evening following dinner the three of them, Jason, Narelle and James were sitting at the dining table enjoying a great bottle of Penfold's Max's *Pinot Noir* and the conversation was about the discovery of the company in Gladstone that morning and what connections the company may have with the owners of the mining lease on Watsonville Station.

Jason had already told Narelle and James about Mark being in Cooktown on behalf of JCE who he was engaged as an analyst for the purpose of feasibility studies.

Mark had told Jason that he was negotiating with Strauss and Watson for the purchase of their station and that they refused to sell their property point blank.

'Well that's all pretty simple' said James who had looked up the prospectus that afternoon for Watsonville Pastoral and Mining. 'They are envisioning a gross profit after only the second year of trading of around forty eight million dollars, that is big dollars when you consider that they only paid around six million for it and the prospectus shows a loan of only twenty million dollars for capital expenditure and breeding stock, that will reduce the capex to nothing after two years, pretty good deal'.

'Yes' said Narelle, 'But when Mark tried to buy it for JCE, it wasn't for sale, so they were going to miss out on those huge profits, so…Mark has put in his report to JCE like you said Jason, that the property is not for sale, then another subsidiary of JCE is in touch with the people on a mining lease on the same property, then Marks goes missing whilst fishing with the same people that the JCE subsidiary was talking to,….Hellooo?' She looked at Jason matter of factly.

'But where is the advantage to JCE by getting Mark off the scene?' asked James.

'JCE's advantage was exactly what has transpired, but it's not a fluke as it appears to be, but it was possibly by design' Narelle added.

Jason had suddenly sat upright with what Narelle had said, my god, she could be right he thought.

'That's it! if something had happened to Strauss and Watson, like death, hypothetically speaking, then the property would go into Strauss and Watson's estates and may still not be available for purchase by JCE,…but..by removing Mark and blaming it on Strauss and Watson by two witnesses, the police arrest the accused Strauss and Watson, once found guilty the police seize the property as a crime scene and then when convicted, the public trust take it over for public disposal..wallah!' said Jason quite confident.

• • • • • • • •

JCE Pty Ltd

James then suggested that his girlfriend's grandfather was a retired company auditor and he may be interested in looking at these companies for us.

Jason pleasantly noted the 'us' in James' suggestion, thinking that at least one other person besides Narelle and himself suspected something was amiss with JCE.

The girlfriend's grandfather turned out to be a retired magistrate who the federal government of Australia once commissioned as an auditor for various government departments and when told the story of Mark Crampton by Jason was more than keen to have a look into the company of Juliet Consolidated Enterprises.

Jason had travelled the two hundred and thirty kilometres to Woodgate Beach, a small community near Bundaberg on the central Queensland coast, to meet Travis Lachlan the grandfather of Amy Lachlan the girlfriend of James.

At seventy five years of age and seemingly very fit and in good health, 'thanks to a good beer' as he commented he enjoyed living by the beach and brewing his own beer.

He and his wife, Wendy, also fit and active were keen bowlers and spent a lot of time at the bowling club and also enjoyed fishing.

Travis had listened intently as Jason told of how he had met with Mark Crampton in Cooktown until he had heard the news of his disappearance on the Monday morning following the events of the previous day.

Travis Lachlan could instantly see the logic portrayed by Jason in the instance of blaming a murder upon the owners of Watsonville Station to gain access to buy the property and he agreed to have a look at JCE and would get back to him with his findings. He also added that he would enjoy doing it immensely as he no longer came across the opportunity of this kind of exercise.

The report from Travis came swiftly and caught Jason by surprise at the expedience.

He had listed the six members on the board of JCE as joint owners of the company and listed their names with a brief description of the person including their personal history.

Of the six members, Travis had described three of them to be of doubtful character. He explained this as quite normal and it is usually the doubtful people that recruit the squeaky clean people to throw a smokescreen for any company audits and/or investigations.

In his report, he made mention of the members whom he had referred to as 'doubtful'.

Father Damien Downes as he was, and thought Travis, still may be a suspect in the drowning of

Bishop Gillard at Canberra. Father Damien was acting as the Bishop's chaperone on the evening of his disappearance and witnesses have reported that the Bishop was last seen with Father Damien, but nothing could be proven at the time, the case, however, has never been closed nor the coroners reported concluded.

Carl Stephenson, who is also the chairman and director of Northern Hotels which also operated a subsidiary called Northern Trading & Logistics of which a Mr Kirill Nikolaev is nominated as the managing director.

Kirill is well known to the police as a leading figure in drug production and distribution. Travis Lachlan could not confirm that Kirill was an illegal migrant

Carl Stephenson stepped down from his position as police commissioner when he was accused in state parliament of being involved in drug production in Far North Queensland in 2014.

Fiona Gibson was also formally the Deputy Premier of Queensland and was basically sacked from that position when Stephenson stepped down as police commissioner.

She is currently being investigated by ASIC (Australian Securities & Investments Commission) for an alleged Ponzi scheme.

An unconfirmed report states that the company, JCE was struggling to meet some leasing commitments with some of its subsidiary companies as well as superannuation payout issues and was at that time desperately seeking a new venture.

Travis had also looked at the case against Strauss and Watson and thought that their defence was inadequate but not necessarily from its administer but possibly from another influence, and he left it to a guess in what capacity, in other words, the barrister appointed by legal aid may have been advised that by being successful in defence may not be prudent to further appointments.

As with the prosecutor proceeding with a case with such limited physical evidence and unreliable witnesses and with a heavy reliance on circumstantial evidence. Strange to say the least he thought.

The former magistrate also believed that the satellite telephone belonging to Jason could be used as new evidence but was most likely not good enough to get the case reopened, besides it probably would have been destroyed by now, looking at the scenario presented by Jason he did however feel that it would not take too much of a police investigation into Andrews and Barnes to come up with some compelling evidence, ideally, if the police could convince the pair to tell the truth, but sadly the police are very limited to the methods of truth seeking allowed to them.

Jason was now convinced that they had been right in assuming that Mark's fishing companions were his likely murderers, but how could he take it further when it seemed that the police had shut down any enquiries into the Crampton disappearance?

He thought that maybe he could get Andrews or Barnes to speak and tell him what happened, or even where Mark's body was, that would be better, especially with the evidence of the sat phone communications which is irrefutable. Jason had an idea and called his old mate from his army days, Les Morton, he called his mobile number.

'This is Les, leave a message' the phone said.

Jason left a message, 'Jason from one R T B Kapooka, call me back on this number.

Jason then called Warren Jackson, the chopper pilot at Cooktown.

'yellow', said a voice after the phone had nearly rang out.

'Jacko'? Said Jason, 'I'm Jason the copper friend of Mark Crampton, we met a couple of times at the Sovereign'

'Orr yeah,..yeah,..Jason and Mark, yeah I remember you'. Warren had said and Jason asked him if he would be in Cooktown in about two weeks' time as he might have a job for him, Warren had said that he should be, not much happening at the moment.

Jason's phone rang and it was Les returning Jason's call.

'Well brother, I was thinking that you might be dead' Les had said as soon as Jason answered.

When Jason had been kicked out of recruit training at Kapooka, Les had gone through training and went on to more training when he went into the SAS and he had only recently retired from the army.

'Are you busy Bro? Are you up for a drive to Cooktown, I can pick you up from Townsville' said Jason.

'When are you talking man?' Les asked.

'Couple of weeks, I can let you know maybe tomorrow'. Jason said.

'Sounds cool man, I've got fuck all to do these days anyway, except drink piss, just tell me when' Les was keen.

Jason's next call was to his former boss at the Cooktown police station, Ken Marsden. Jason had been unsure of whether to include Ken into his Cooktown meeting, but the more he thought about it the better the idea, he thought as Ken was pretty clued up to police operations and any advice that he may offer would be invaluable to Jason's plan.

Ken answered the phone almost immediately and listened to what Jason had to say which was basically if he could meet up with him in Cooktown one day and then he mentioned briefly what it was about. Jason had been careful to tell Ken just enough about the plan to the extent that if he agreed to meet up with Jason then he knew that he would help him.

Ken said that he would look forward to meeting up with Jason and just to give him a good day's notice.

Jason had collected Les from Townsville on his way from Monto and they were enjoying a get together talk on their way up to Cooktown. They had bypassed Cairns by turning towards Atherton at Mourilyan and towards the last part of the eight hours of the journey Jason had gone into more detail with Les and had said that if Ken wasn't too keen on the idea then it would not go ahead, Les was even more excited about the 'mission' as he then called it and hoped the other dude liked the idea.

Jason had booked two rooms at the Sovereign for five days as he had no idea how long they would need.

They had me up with Warren Jackson on the second night they were there and Jason basically had three questions for him

How many passengers could he take in his helicopter?

Did he know where the Andrews, Barnes mining lease was?

Could he fly Les and himself into the mining lease undetected?

Jason felt that he could detect that Warren was not too sure of what Jason was asking him to do and was about to decline, so Jason told him the theory of what he and his friends had put together about Strauss and Watson being innocent and that he was hoping that the boys Andrews and Barnes might help him to prove it.

Warren gave Jason an unbelieving look and after a little pause said that he was in and for free, there would be no charge for the chopper,

'Those fellers were me mates Jason, and I knew that they would not do that to Mark, they could be pricks for sure, but not fucking murderers, I'm in all the way' Warren committed. 'I can take both of yous in the chopper no worries and a bit of gear, I know the lease well and have flown over it a hundred times and I can land you just down river where the wind always blows down from the hut so no one will hear me coming'.

Warren said that he wanted only a day's notice to fuel up and was happy to do a recce out there first to make sure the pricks were there. 'Shit' Jason thought to himself, he hadn't thought of the possibility of Andrews and Barnes not being out there at the lease.

Ken arrived and had dinner with Jason and Les and they then had a few beers afterwards, it was at that time Jason exposed his plan of getting a confession of sorts from Andrews and Barnes.

Ken had at first said it was a stupid idea, and then he said it was stupid but with merit and then after a short pause, said that it would possibly work and then asked what did Jason want Ken to do to make this plan work, he then told Jason that these two arseholes had taunted him for quite a while.

Ken whilst a police officer had suspected a drug plantation out at the lease and after considerable investigation work had determined it to be an illegal coca growing operation and had contacted his boss at Mareeba to discuss his plan of a raid and to source backup.

He was told that a plan on a raid for marijuana could go ahead but to leave the coca alone as it would be part of a much bigger planned raid down the track to expose bigger drug operatives.

Ken, believing what he had been told had organised a raid with backup police from Mareeba and discovered that the growers were not there on the day of the raid, he suspected that they had been tipped off, and that coca plants were in abundance but very few marijuana plants to even warrant a raid. Then in the subsequent months when no raid on the coca plantation had happened, he questioned his boss with respect to this and was basically told to mind his own business.

To say that Ken was disillusioned was certainly an understatement and he thought seriously about blowing the whistle on his boss but thought about other people, for instance, a police sergeant in another Queensland town who had gone missing for no apparent reason and he was not the only one. Ken then retired from the police force.

The three of them were staying at the hotel and it was two am when the door to Jason's room was opened by two uniformed Australian Federal Police officers, who woke Jason up and placed handcuffs on his wrists behind his back whilst telling him 'To take it easy, he was being detained'.

He was taken downstairs and into the rear car park where a Landcruiser wagon was waiting, he was placed into the back seat to join Ken and Les, also in handcuffs.

The Landcruiser left the hotel and drove to the Cooktown airport on Endeavour Valley road about ten kilometres from town where a Gulfstream G280 jet aircraft was waiting. They were placed on board and were separated around the ten seat aircraft. The time from takeoff to landing was all of fifteen minutes.

Another Landcruiser wagon was waiting on the tarmac at Cairns Airport and took them to the AFP headquarters at the airport where they were placed into separate interview rooms.

'I'm Superintendent Peter James' the man wearing jeans and a polo shirt addressed Jason, 'I know that you are Jason Walsh and you had intentions of raiding the mining lease of Terry Andrew and David Barnes, is that correct?' Jason saw that there was also another man wearing casual clothes sitting on a chair by the office door as he answered.

'Yes,…but what is going on here'.

'Can you tell me your intentions for the raid' the superintendent asked, 'And relax! You are not under arrest, we just want to talk to you'.

Jason told Peter James about Mark Campton and his going missing and about the sat phone and his belief that Andrews and Barnes had something to do with Mark's disappearance and that he believed that somehow a company called JCE is connected with another company Northern Trading and Logistics who have been communicating with Andrews and Barnes at the mining lease.

'I suppose the bottom line is that I wanted to get some answers' Jason concluded.

Peter James was fully aware of the missing Mark Crampton and his department shared similar views to that of Jason Walsh, the AFP however was restricted in the deployment of truth extraction.

'What makes you think that these two guys are going to tell you anything?' Peter James wanted to know.

One of my team is an ex SAS linguist, he spent quite some time in Afghanistan talking with soldiers from the Taliban and if they can tell him what he wants to know, then I am sure that Andrews and Barns would also tell my man what I want to know'. Jason went on to tell the Federal police officer that he was hoping to find the location of Mark's body and then he would hand it over to the Queensland police, but he wasn't sure where as he believed the officer in charge at Mareeba did not want to know anything about it.

'We are aware that you are ex police as with one other of your group, and that you are well aware that what you intend to do is against the law and you could all be prosecuted for such an act' the superintendent told Jason.

Jason, looking at the officer asked 'What has any of this got to do with the federal police?'

Superintendent James told Jason that the AFP has been closely working with various state police in relation to a huge drug operation that extends to North Queensland and beyond.

They have been closely monitoring Northern Trading and Logistics and are also aware of its ties to a company known as JCE. They have been focused on the cultivation of drugs and not the disappearance of Mark Crampton, although they are fully aware of the case. Peter James went on to say that he was also aware that the company, Northern Trading also has a contact at a local police station and provides restricted information back to them in relation to police activities.

Peter James then shocked Jason by inviting him and his two colleagues along on the raid in a limited capacity, that is to interview the occupants at the Watsonville mining lease with respect to the disappearance of Mark Crampton. But if anyone asks, it never happened.

They were flown back to Cooktown with instructions to be at a designated place and at a designated time that morning where they were then flown by Polair to the mining lease.

The Watsonville mining lease was already under the control of a police swat team which included some members of the AFP when Jason, Ken and Les arrived.

An AFP officer met them at the helicopter landing zone which was about one hundred meters from the lease.

The officer told them that they had approximately fifty minutes to conduct their interview and that he would be just outside if he was wanted and gave them swat team masks to put on with the instruction 'not to remove them'.

The three of them went into the main shed to find both Andrews and Barnes handcuffed and leg shackled sitting on plastic kitchen chairs in the centre of the shed.

Les went in search of a bucket and a towel which he soon found, he then filled the bucket with water and within seven minutes Barnes had told them that he would show them where the body of Mark Crampton was, Andrews just glared at him. Jason had recorded the interview with his phone.

Jason spoke to the officer outside the door and he organised a vehicle to take one of the Qld police officers with two AFP officers and Barnes to the location and ordered Jason, Ken and Les back on board the helicopter where they were taken back to Cooktown.

It was early afternoon by the time they got back to Cooktown and they walked from the oval where the Polair helicopter had dropped them over to the hotel where they were staying and, still in a sort of shock from the morning's events, went into the bar for a drink.

They would all love to know what was happening just now at the mining lease site but they realised that they would most likely hear nothing for a while and that they could not talk about it to anyone.

Between them, they discussed what had happened that morning and thought what a fluke that had been with the AFP about to do a raid just before their planned attack on Andrews and Barnes, and how Barnes had broken before Les had even started to apply the 'water treatment' to him. And then Jason asked,

'How did they know, how did the AFP know that we were planning to go to the Watsonville mining lease?'

Jason ordered another beer just as Ken said that the only other person who knew was Warren Jackson.

Could it be that Warren was a member of the AFP, or worked for them? They came to the unanimous conclusion that was the case with his great cover of flying all over the properties with cattle mustering and power transmission spotting.

'He was spotting alright' said Les, 'And reporting it straight back to the AFP'.

• • • • • • • •

Epilogue

It was more than two weeks since the morning of the AFP raid on the Watsonville mining lease raid and there was no mention in the media of a drug plantation raid nor any mention about the discovery of the body of Mark Crampton. Jason was becoming concerned that perhaps David Barnes had changed his mind about showing the police where Mar Crampton's body was hidden.

He was considering trying to contact the AFP officer Peter James but was wholly aware that he had been told that the Cooktown morning event did not happen, and he then realised that other operations were likely to be connected to that raid and it may be months before any public information may be released. It was never released.

Jason answered the call, it was James congratulating him,

'Congratulations?' said Jason, confused and asked James what was he talking about.

'On the news!' James replied, 'About Stan Strauss and David Watson being released from prison'.

Jason turned on his television and went to channel 22 for the ABC news but there was no mention of any prison release, he looked at the latest news on his laptop and 9News was reporting that *The two men who were found guilty of the murder of Mark Crampton over four years ago have been released from prison due to the discovery of new evidence and that no further details were available just yet.*

Just as Jason was about to close his laptop he noticed another news article, *'ACT Police cold case reopened' Police. Police have new evidence in the decades old case of the drowning of Bishop Gillard in Lake Burley Griffin. Father Damien Downe is assisting police with their enquiries.*

It was during the course of the next seven months that more 'breaking news' stories began to emerge about the resignation of the Queensland premier and following that by about a month, the resignation of the Queensland police commissioner.

It seemed to be well spaced out in the media releases and after six months came the news that a former director of the Queensland based company, Northern Hotels was jailed for fraud. Some months later, an article about a Russian nationalist who was charged with drug offences in Gladstone.

Jason and his friends must have all missed the press release of two men remanded in custody for the murder of a man in Far Northern Queensland and went on to say that they are expected to stand trial in two years' time.

It was all very quiet and low key, even the compensation payment from the Queensland Government to Strauss and Watson was only a snippet advising that the pair had accepted an undisclosed amount.

The End.